Interstellar
Objects

A
Science Fiction
Anthology

Dillon Sienko

Cover artwork designed by Andy Jacques

www.ajacquesphotography.com

For more by Dillon Sienko, visit:
www.dillonsienko.com

For my family and friends, Luna, Vega, and Mels

Contents

Somnambulist 1

The Beginning of the Beginning of Us as We Know It 31

The Golden Spiral 38

Sols of Our Lives 52

Aurora 71

☉2761 /III 78

In the Monuments of the Valley 97

Ditto 113

Unbound, Unchained 128

The Disappearance of Casey Flack 132

The End of the End of Us as We Know It 152

Humanity 172

Somnambulist

Ava's staccato breaths echoed throughout the cold corridor. She fumbled through the small pack strapped to her right thigh, searching for the gauze she knew came standard with each one. She yanked it hard from the pack and unfurled it in front of her. She wrapped the white gauze tight around her hand. She bit down hard and fought off the desire to scream as the fabric was pulled tight against where her ring finger and pinky used to be. The white of the wrap quickly turned red but she hoped it would be enough to control the bleeding for now.

Ava sat on the smooth floor with her back against the wall. The dim backup lights of the hall were barely bright enough for her to see a few feet in front of her. She laid her head back against the metal and tried to calm herself with deep, heavy breaths. She was tired, so very tired. *Maybe if I close my eyes now I can just sleep this all away*, she thought. She wanted nothing more than to drift into a dark, peaceful nothing, putting her waking nightmare behind her. Her shoulders fell, her eyelids slowly shut. She could feel her consciousness begin to slip away into the arms of a deep, dreamless sleep.

A clang reverberated throughout the corridor, deep in her bones. The sharp sound was followed by a guttural, anguished scream. Her eyes sprung open and she immediately hated herself for giving in to her body. It was coming. She had to move.

Ava rose to her feet as quickly as her slowing muscles allowed. She stabilized herself against the wall then pushed off towards the door at the other end. She pressed her thumb against the scanner to the left of the door at the end of the hall, but nothing happened. She pulled her thumb off and pressed again, this time for longer, but there was still no response.

"Damn power outages," she muttered to herself. "Come on, come on, come on. Work, you piece of shit!" She slammed her hand against the side of the box. The sound was growing closer behind her. She could hear it against the door at the beginning of the hall. She had closed it when she entered the space, but that wouldn't stop it. Ava knew it would do nothing but slow it down for a few brief, valuable moments.

"Access denied. Invalid authentication," she could hear the overhead speakers in the previous room say. It was trying to get through.

Thankfully, as an engineer, she had her own

tricks. She reached underneath the bottom lip of the panel in front of her. With a quick upwards pressure, she dislodged a small cover and exposed a tight grouping of wires. She bent down to get a better look, but the lights were too dim to distinguish any color.

"Access denied. Invalid authentication," she heard again. It wouldn't take much longer for it to figure it out and open the door.

She weaseled the index and middle fingers of her right hand into the small wire compartment and let them search the space for what she hoped was the correct wire. They varied slightly in thickness and so she let that guide what would inevitably be a mostly hopeful guess. If she pulled the wrong wire, the door would lock for good. She'd be trapped.

"Access granted." With a beep and the sound of a metal lock shifting, the door at the beginning of the hall behind her began to open. The raspy shrieks from behind it suddenly grew louder.

"Now or never, Ava!" She let her fingers tighten on a wire and yanked downwards. Sparks flew from the bottom of the thumb pad's panel and onto Ava's boots. The panel made a series of quick sounds as if it was deciding on Ava's passage.

She didn't want to look back. It was getting closer. Its inhuman sounds had finally entered the corridor. Ava watched the computer make its decision. Finally, she was welcomed with a familiar beep and the sound of shifting metal. Her door began to swing open.

She squeezed through as soon as it was open wide enough and slammed the emergency shut button on the panel on the other side. The heavy door squealed to a halt and then began to move back in the other direction. She chose once more not to look back down the long hallway. Instead, she continued forward down a short hallway until she reached a fork. She could move up a tight, rusted metal staircase that spiraled upwards into darkness or continue down a secondary shaft to her left. She pondered for a split second but the sound of shifting air and squeaking metal from the door she had just closed told her that it had somehow made its way through. It motivated a quick decision, and she bolted towards her right. Grabbing the black metal railing of the stairs as stabilization, she moved upwards fast. Her motions were fueled by adrenaline but also encumbered by the exhaustion racking her body and the intense pain in her left hand. It felt as if her arms were doing more work pulling herself up using the railing than her legs were doing pushing off each step.

The staircase eventually opened into a small space filled with containers, likely one of the food stores. Some had clearly been opened in a hurry, their contents ravaged. Ava pushed past the boxes to the manual door at the other end of the room. The manual doors, while providing access not limited by status, also provided a more secure and reliable way of locking the door. Gripping hard, she spun the locking wheel mounted to the center of the door until she heard the click of the lock letting go. She heaved the door open, applying pressure with her shoulders, and moved into the next area, slamming the door closed behind her. She spun the wheel all the way until she heard the click of the lock, then pulled down hard on a set of levers to the right of the door, locking it from the other side. It wouldn't prevent it from getting to her, but it would force it to go another way, and that was good enough for now.

She finally felt some semblance of security, even if she knew it would likely only be for a short time. The previous few days of running and hiding had done little to provide context for the nightmare she and the rest of the crew were living.

Ava had been separated from her fellow engineers since the power outages had begun, and as each day passed and as she struggled to keep ahead of the terror that stalked her from one end of the station to the other, she grew increasingly uneasy in not being able to find anyone. She also had no clue what that thing was or where it came from. She pushed the thought to the back of her head, as she had done countless times over the previous dozen hours, and brought her attention to her current situation.

She suddenly found herself in the pitch black. Despite the commonplace creaks of shifting metal that she had long since grown accustomed to, Ava was shrouded in silence. It was ominous, but it meant that her pursuer was no longer in tow. Either she had lost it completely or it had turned around, but either way, she was currently alone.

As an engineer, Ava hadn't spent much time in these rooms, but she was fairly certain she now stood in what was essentially a glorified supply closet. To conserve power, even backup systems were cut off for these rooms unless the room's circuit was on, so she knew finding the power would at least provide some light.

She shimmied along the wall, her outstretched arms acting as feelers to guide her way. After only 10 or so feet, her hand collided with what felt like a rusted lever. She pawed around the panel it was attached to confirm her suspicions and then pulled down. A high-pitched hum sounded from the panel and the backup lights in the room came on, providing a much-needed illumination.

Ava was indeed standing in a supply room, but it was mostly lacking in actual supplies. The room was in a state of chaos. Objects thrown about, containers in various states of disarray. It had likely been looted at the beginning of all of this, and a thin layer of undisturbed dust had already begun to settle on everything, so she knew the room hadn't been visited since.

She spent a few minutes salvaging what she could. A small flashlight, batteries included. A second medical pack, which she strapped to her leg below the first. Two protein bars, one of which she ate and which provided the first sustenance she had had in almost two days.

While the rations would help keep her body going for a little longer, Ava was admittedly disappointed she hadn't found anything particularly useful in her continued fight for survival. She flipped and searched every crate, every box, but there was nothing. Except, she knew she was missing something. She'd been in these storage spaces before. She knew the importance of the cabling that ran along its walls, and she knew there was often a fairly foolproof method for severing the connections of those cables stored somewhere in the room.

She peered around, searching for some sign of a hidden cabinet along the metal walls. After a few moments of searching, she found an old-school, heavily rusted lock placed through a small metal loop protruding along the slightly raised edge of a panel around eye-height. She didn't have the key, but she didn't need it.

Ava picked up the heaviest but easiest the grasp container she could find amongst those strewn about her and swung it as hard as she could at the lock. A billow of amber-colored flakes exploded off of it, but the lock held solid. She swung again, and then again, until finally the lock cracked at its hinges and fell to the ground. She threw the container to the side and pried open the panel. A hatchet, browned with age but otherwise exactly what she was hoping for, hung from a hook inside the inset cabinet. She pulled it down, admired it for a moment, and then placed it in her belt.

Another manual door provided her exit, which she locked like the last once she made it out of the room. This new hallway branched off innumerably into additional hallways and rooms.

She needed a way to contact someone, anyone that would listen. An assortment of faceplates were attached to a small area on the wall in front of her, pointing in the direction of various rooms and labs. Medbay, Crew Lounge, Survey Lab, Mess Hall, Crew Quarters, Research Ops, Engineering. She had just come from Engineering. While they had once had a long-distance communication device, it had since been destroyed. It had appeared to Ava as though someone had destroyed it, deliberately, but in her attempt to fix the device, it attacked her. She had yet to truly ponder who would have willingly damaged one of their only means of communication with the outside, and she had more pressing matters to attend to for the time being. The survey lab, on the other hand, would have one, and hopefully still in working condition. Ava followed the direction of the arrow and continued left down the hallway.

She moved quickly but with a horrified caution. She gripped the hatchet hard in her right hand. The exhaustion acted as a constant reminder to keep moving. If she stopped, she feared nothing now could keep her from sleep, from giving in to whatever would take her to oblivion.

As she rounded the wide curve in the hall, passing the medbay first and then the mess hall—both of which appeared empty through the darkness—Ava couldn't help but wonder where everyone was. She hadn't seen anyone, alive or dead, since Engineering. While the crew wasn't very large, their complete and utter absence was unsettling.

An odd light from around the bend caught her attention. Its existence wasn't particularly strange, rather, what made it odd was that it was *natural* light. In all of the time she had spent in the station, she often forgot that there were a few locations that allowed her access to light from the outside. It illuminated 12 large, fading letters painted onto the sheet metal walls of the hallway.

SOMNAMBULIST

The name of the station, her home away from home.

She saw the source of the light as she cleared the corner. A circular porthole-style window sat eye-height up the wall at the end of the hall. She moved quickly down the corridor until she made it to the faceplate hanging to the left of the window. "Survey Lab" was written in bold typeface with a skinny arrow pointing to the left. On the next line, "Research Ops" pointed to the right down a short hall.

She turned to continue towards the survey lab

but felt drawn towards the window directly in front of her. Perhaps she never truly took the time to look out the few windows she had access to. The view often made her feel small. Insignificant. She regularly had to remind herself that what they were doing was important. It mattered to the people outside that window.

She peered out at the blackness of space. The vastness provided the same crushing feeling as always. She had to draw her attention away from the nothingness to rein in the cold, claustrophobic feeling crawling up her spine.

Instead, she looked down at the planet floating in the void below her. The hemisphere facing her was shrouded in darkness. The system's sun was on the other side of the planet, shining into the station and providing the natural light that was illuminating the corridor. Even at this distance, the lights covering the massive landmasses of Earth-Two were exceptionally bright in the darkness. It was hard to find any bit of land that was not covered in them. Little yellow ants crawling across a great blue-green marble. A reminder of this station's purpose.

Many years of overpopulation had eaten up the world's resources. Missions like this harvested and processed rare materials, minerals, and resources from Soror—the planet's only moon—and near-planet asteroids, as was the case with Ava's mission. As an engineer, she worked to keep the boat afloat. It was a dirty, unglamorous job, but Ava convinced herself it was better than living down there. The people down there were suffering far worse.

A flurry of metallic sounds resonated down the hall to her right. They were coming from behind the door to the research ops lab. She tightened her already vice-like grip on the hatchet and moved towards the door. A cold sweat grew on her forehead.

Ava had access to most rooms on the station as an engineer for use in the case of a station-wide emergency. Such occurrences were uncommon, but she was deeply thankful the past few days that Command had provided her with the additional access nonetheless. That freedom had allowed a mostly unhindered journey throughout the station. The exception to this, unfortunately in this case, had always been the research ops lab. Even if the power outages hadn't been messing with the access pads, Ava wouldn't have had the correct authorization. Few people had knowledge of what actually happened inside of the lab, and fewer still had access to the room itself. *It was a mining mission, what could they possibly have to hide?* was the common sentiment amongst the crew. Nonetheless, their privacy was generally respected and engineers like Ava were kept in the dark.

Today was not a normal day, though. Assuming that her pursuer was still back the way she had come, the sounds from inside the room were likely caused by one of the ship's human occupants. It would be a welcome sight.

She popped open the bottom panel, yanked the wire to short the door lock, and waited as it began to swing open.

There were no backup lights in this room. Instead, red emergency lights blinked on and off, bathing the room in periodic, intense, bloody shadow. A small cabinet and its contents laid strewn across the floor some feet from the door. Ava held the hatchet at the ready. She slowly moved into the space, scanning the shadows for any sign of recent life.

The walls were lined with workbenches that were covered in devices and instruments whose purpose Ava could only guess at. They appeared to crawl in the flashing lights. The shadows would grow intensely and dance before the lights blinked out, then repeat their dance as the lights returned. The hair on Ava's neck stood on end. *Something* had knocked that cabinet down and made the sounds she had heard from the hallway. This room had one way out as far as she could tell. Whatever it was, it was still here.

"Hello?" she whispered nervously. "Anyone here? I won't hurt you. Just come on out." Nothing. "Please, my name is Ava Orton. I'm an engineer. I just wa—"

A shadow shifted, then grew, then diffused entirely as a small man came crawling out from behind one of the tall supply containers that was leaning against the lab's far wall. Ava threw her bandaged left hand up and open wide. She winced with pain but hoped the gesture and bloody wound would convince the man that she was not a threat, that she was simply another victim of the madness.

"Please don't hurt me," he said. His voice was pleading but not frightened.

"Hey, no one's going to hurt you," Ava said back, sliding the hatchet handle back into her belt. "Is it just you? Is there anyone else?" She peered around the room, but he shook his head. She kept the door she had entered through open. *Just for good measure*, she thought. She gestured towards the one table in the room. She flipped two overturned chairs and sat in one of them. The right sleeve of the man's lab coat was torn. "Are you alright? Are you injured?" she asked.

"Injured?" he asked, confused at her question. "Oh, no, not injured," he responded, peering down at his sleeve and recognizing the motivation for the question. "Cabinet fell and caught my sleeve. Accident."

He sat down in the other chair. The deep grooves in his taught face were scarily obvious in the stark red light. Ava reached into her small pack and pulled out the second protein bar for him, which he ate with a ferocity that made clear he had likely not eaten since everything went to hell a few days before.

"Where is everyone else?" Ava asked. He considered his response for a few seconds as he swallowed the last bite.

"Not here. They've...gone."

"Gone where? I've been from one end of the ship to the other. I've seen evidence of looting, of pain, but no evidence of where anyone is or has gone."

"They made their decisions." His tone was calm and reasonable, but his words made Ava feel uncomfortable.

"Doctor, where are your colleagues? Do you know where the crew is?" she asked, frustrated.

"You know, Miss Orton," the grey-haired scientist in front of her said with a tone both sincere and condescending, "I have been around a long time. I have seen the worst of our kind do some of the worst things you can imagine and likely much that you cannot. I have seen the brink of human consciousness and the horrors of which it is capable," he said, pausing for a moment. Ava stared at him, unsure what to say. "Did you look out that window before you found me?" She nodded. "Then you see what has become of our planet. We have done that to ourselves. We have ruined our home. It is why we are here, up in our lonely orbit."

"Yes, Doctor, to mine resources, I know." Ava was becoming increasingly more impatient, but before she could interject further, the doctor continued on.

"Mining...yes. Of course. Iron, tungsten, nickel, ammonia. Provide for them what they can no longer provide for themselves. But, tell me, Miss Orton—do you mind if I call you Ava?" Ava nodded in approval. "Have you ever actually believed that our attempts up here could truly help those below? These are scraps.

We're only delaying the inevitable." With that he stood and moved towards a bank of computers along one of the lab walls.

"I'm only a station engineer," she said. "We'd always been told our mission was part of something important. To help the billions down there. That we were making a difference. Who am I to question that?"

"Oh, we are, Ava. We are making a difference. Just not the way you or the world believes."

"What is that supposed to mean?" She asked, confused.

"You have seen *it* haven't you?" He asked. He gestured towards her bandaged hand. "It did that?" She squirmed and stared down at the bloody gauze and her missing digits.

"Yeah...I've seen it. From my escape..." she said, referencing the hand. "What the fuck is that thing...that horrible thing moving through the ship?" He was faced away from her, staring at the black screens of the computers.

"It knows. It's growing smarter." He mumbled almost exclusively to himself.

"What does it know?"

"The others didn't seem to understand. They couldn't comprehend what it was capable of."

"The others? Do you mean the other researchers?" The cold sweat was beginning to return to her forehead. "Where are they, Doctor?" He continued to face away from her.

"They told me I was wrong about it, that I was crazy. They told me we should have killed it before it got this far. But they couldn't see what I could. I can feel it inside of me, this...this light. I have it, and *it* has it, but they didn't, so I gave them the choice." Ava stood slowly. She could feel the constricting tightness in her spine again. The claustrophobia, the smallness.

"Doctor...where are the other scientists? Where is the rest of the crew?" Her tone became sharp and her hand migrated towards the hatchet.

"I gave them the choice. Assimilate, or go home. Most of them chose home." *Home?*

She had noticed on her journey here from across the station that the two small transport shuttles, meant to ferry crew short hops from station to station, were missing. She remembered how angry it had made her when she saw it. *Assholes left without me.* But the shuttles were only temporary transport. The only way back to Earth-Two from the Somnambulist was to take a shuttle from here to Callisto Station, and then a shuttle from there to Aristides Station, which acted as the main hub for the mining stations and had the necessary space vehicles to get crew back to Earth-Two.

"You sent them away on the shuttles? To go back to Earth-Two?"

"Oh no, not back down to the planet. I mean the *original* home of all things." He typed a few characters on the keyboard in front of him. The set of screens in front of him came to life. *I thought there was no power,* Ava thought to herself. *Must be on some sort of secondary backup for the lab.*

He typed in an additional set of commands and two video playbacks opened on a pair of screens. Ava moved closer towards the small monitors to get a better look. It appeared to be recorded footage from the security cameras inside of the two shuttles. In each shuttle sat six white-coated scientists. There was no sound, but the nervous and unsure looks on their faces and the apparent rapid discussion between them told Ava that they were clearly on edge. The scientists shook as the shuttles launched from the bay. Ava expected them both to turn right sharply after leaving the bay towards Callisto Station, but they instead turned left. *Terminus Station, maybe,* she thought as she watched the footage. Except they kept turning left, away from the planet, then away from the direction of Terminus Station. They were headed towards nothing. They were headed straight into deep space. It sank in, and Ava could barely keep herself from falling to the ground in shock.

"You killed them. You told them you were sending them home, but you killed them. You locked the controls and you left them to starve in space." She was breathing hard.

"I gave them the choice." He said coolly.

"And those that weren't on those shuttles? Where is the rest of the crew? The surveyors, the engineers? My friends?!"

The doctor sighed. He stepped away from the computers and towards a group of stacked containers to his left.

"Where are they?!" She was shouting now.

He began to unstack the containers, pulling each to the ground and moving them aside. Ava noticed something that she hadn't before as the bottom most container was shifted away from the wall. In the red flashing light, the dark stain on the metal floor around those boxes was previously difficult to see. The longer she stared, the more clearly a picture began to form in her head. The doctor moved towards the barren wall behind where the boxes were stacked. The stain seemed to originate from behind the wall. He placed his hands a few feet apart at shoulder height and pushed. A segment of the wall, roughly seven feet high and three feet wide, popped inwards. Rancid air blew into the lab from the space behind it and Ava had to keep herself from vomiting. The doctor stepped back as the section slid sideways, disappearing behind the wall next to it.

This new space was surprisingly large. It was at least as big as the lab, but Ava had no clue it had existed. It had never appeared on any of the station's schematics. It didn't exist, yet here it was. Unlike the remainder of the base, this room had full power. It was brightly lit by stark-white overhead lights, and there was no denying what had caused the dark stains on the lab floor.

Bodies laid strewn about the metal floor. They were torn up, shredded, ripped apart. They no longer entirely resembled humans but rather just singular parts of some greater whole. Despite the carnage, Ava recognized the surveyor suits, the command personnel uniforms, and the industrial shirts and pants of the engineers. They were the same as the ones Ava was currently wearing. A large operating table, much larger than necessary for a human, took up much of the floor space at the back of the room. It was soaked in bloody bits, both mechanical and flesh, but was otherwise empty.

She felt unable to react. She couldn't cry or get angry or lash out. She just stared at those people. The longer she stared, the more *it* made sense. The physical appearance of her terrible stalker had horrified and confused her, but she had not once stopped to truly consider its existence. She had only tried to survive. But now, looking at the madness in front of her, it made sense.

"You did this. You made that thing!" Despite the pain in her left hand, she could feel it ball up into a half-fist. The muscles in her back grew taught and twitched with readiness. The doctor moved nonchalantly from the opening of the new room back towards the computers, despite her clearly aggressive stance.

"At first it was born of metal. We gave it a mechanical body, something physical so it could learn about its world outside of the computer. A babe in the universe. But it cried out, it pained. The human side of it could not comprehend its new cold existence. I needed to make it comfortable, to make it understand what it was like to live, so I gave it flesh. But it wasn't enough. It's never enough. The more I give, the smarter it becomes. And the more anguished it becomes as well."

That cabinet didn't fall by accident. He knew I'd come when I heard it. Ava had begun moving back towards the open door to the lab.

"It needs more. Can't you see, Ava?" He once again began typing commands into the computer. "We are not long for the universe. Humans have had their time. There must be the next step, the next form of our own existence!" His tone was becoming ecstatic.

Ava reached the door but was shocked to see it close fast and hard in front of her.

She turned back towards the doctor. The screens around him were now filled with live feeds from all around the station. Most showed the same thing. Dimly lit hallways, empty labs, storage rooms. Silence. But movement on one screen caught her eye. It was blurry, but the motion was unmistakable. It was the doctor's horrible creation, lumbering past the camera. It disappeared from frame, then reappeared shortly after in another. Then another. The third feed she recognized as the beginning of the long curving hallway with the window. Somehow, the doctor was leading it right to them.

"It'll kill us both, Doctor! We're the only two left. It won't care if you created it or not!" Ava pulled the hatchet from her belt and held it shakily at her side as she faced the door. "You've trapped it here by sending the shuttles away. We are the last assimilations that will ever happen," she said sharply as she turned her head back towards him.

The doctor turned on another screen. Six bright red letters flashed large across the screen. MAYDAY. He'd sent out a network-wide distress signal, calling for help. Soon there'd be shuttles from multiple stations descending on the Somnambulist. Presuming *it* could assimilate the right knowledge, it could figure out how to get to everyone else. To Earth-Two.

"What have you done..." Ava muttered, exhausted, not entirely capable of understanding the nightmare occurring around her.

"Can't you feel it? The light...it's growing brighter for us!" He stared back at her with wild eyes but then turned back towards the computers.

"Don't open that fucking door!" she yelled. She ran over to the doctor and pulled him back hard by the lapel of his lab coat. He fell to the ground and hit his head against one of the containers he had previously moved. Blood started flowing from a gash on the back of his head and he was clearly disoriented. "I don't want to kill you, Doctor, but I will. If it means this'll end!" she sputtered at him as she stood over his crumpled body with the hatchet held high.

"It's too late," he muttered through a spat of coughs. "It's done."

A beep sounded from the door and it was soon followed by a mechanical click. It started to open. She ran at it, throwing her shoulder into it hard, hoping her rubber-soled boots would provide her traction against the smooth metal floor. She knew better, though. She had repaired these doors all over the ship. She knew she had no chance. It slid her back with ease as it swung inwards.

Ava let go and recoiled back into the room. There was no hiding now. Nothing to cower behind, nowhere to run.

At first it was just the sound of heavy, uneven steps. Then it was the anguished, gurgling cries she had so intensely feared the last few days. Then, from the connecting hallway, a horrid amalgamation—its arm—appeared and grasped onto the corner of the small hall leading to the research ops lab. The rest of its horrific body followed, lumbering awkwardly, heavily, around the corner and down the hall towards the lab.

It was a gruesome terror. A stitched together Frankenstein's monster of human limbs and pieces. Its arms and legs were made up of many human arms and legs. Its chest was wrapped in flesh from who knows what part of Ava's friends and coworkers. Its head was a bulbous mass of flesh covered in eyes and ears, dozens of each, which circumnavigated the entire bloody mess above its neck, providing it with a 360-degree observation of the world. The metal of its endoskeleton could be seen in small bits and patches across its body.

Its massive eight-foot-tall body left disfigured, bloody footprints as it walked. It existed as the purest form of fear.

It screamed wildly. Its eyes, those on the front side of its head, looked directly at Ava. It began to move slowly in her direction, but the doctor, who had since managed to pull himself off the ground, placed himself in between the two.

"It's so bright! The light...can't you see it, Ava?! Salvation!" he screamed wildly. "Set us free!" the doctor yelled as he lunged forward at his horrible abomination. It reacted far quicker than Ava could have possibly expected. It swung its right arm hard and fast at the doctor's head, which nearly exploded on impact. The force sent his body off towards the side, but the creature's left arm grabbed him before he could hit the ground. With its right arm again, the beast threw its mass of fists straight into the doctor's chest, tearing a gaping hole straight through and pushing most of the doctor's insides out his back towards Ava. She jumped back hard, flinching at the shocking nature of the doctor's demise.

It pulled its arm back out and let out what could have been either a triumphant or pained yell as its creator's mangled body fell lifeless to the ground. Its eyes then returned to Ava. She had no interest in feeding its increasing knowledge or body. Wasting no time, she ran fast towards it. As she was hoping, it responded much the same way as it had when the doctor attempted his sacrifice. It swung its arm wide, which she ducked under easily. She swung the hatchet with everything she could muster as she threw herself into an awkward slide between its legs. Some of the human feet which had been attached up the length of its leg kicked out wildly at Ava, but her weapon connected with its target. She buried it deep into what was, for all intents and purposes, its knee, and she could tell she hit metal. It screamed viciously as Ava scrambled past it into the small hallway outside the lab.

She knew her attack only acted as a flesh wound and would do little to harm the creature, but it was enough to slow its pursuit as she moved fast towards the main hallway. She had two options, both of them unpleasant. The first option was to keep running and hiding until she eventually, hopefully found a working comms device to call off-ship, warn those responding to the mayday, and get help. The second option was to go across the hall to the survey lab, which had a comms device but only had one way in or out. She'd be trapped.

Wait, she thought to herself. *That's not the only way out of the survey lab.* She knew she had to decide. She peered back towards the research ops lab as the nightmare aimed its many eyes towards her and turned to follow.

Ava ran down the short hallway in front of her. Popping up the little panel and pulling on the wires, she opened the lab door. She ran into the room and hit the emergency close button behind her. She knew that, either through assimilated knowledge of the ship or through sheer strength, the creature would have no issue making it through the door. She wasted no time.

The survey lab was likely the largest space in the entire station. As the primary lab of the surveyors and miners on the Somnambulist, it contained huge machinery and pieces of equipment, as well as assorted testing and processing machines. Ava had been in the room quite a few times but had little idea what most of the equipment did. In this case, she only needed one particular device.

A heavy pounding at the lab door had begun. Time was short. She raced over to a large cabinet and input a short numeric code. Tall vertical doors opened with a hiss, and a long track slid out horizontally from the top of the opening. A dozen or so green and grey space suits hung from the track, each swinging lightly on their hooks. They were worn by miners and surveyors when making EVA trips outside the confines of the station to study, mine, or survey material that had been caught near the station. Ava wouldn't be using it the same way, but she assumed it would work well enough for her purposes. She pulled the suit on quickly and placed the egg-shaped helmet over her head, snapping it into place. The quick pressurization of the suit made her briefly lightheaded, but she shook it off. She grabbed a pile of thick straps that lay on a utility table next to the cabinet and ran towards the other side of the lab. She had never worn one of the miners' suits but was surprised at how little it restricted her movement compared to the awkward EVA suits of the engineers.

The banging on the door was growing more intense, angrier. Each hit sounded louder than the last, and she could see dents forming on the door.

Ava ran up to a long device sitting atop a tripod. A mining laser. She pulled the tripod close to a wall opposite the doorway to the lab. She wrapped two of the thick straps around her midsection and then tied them tightly around piping lining the wall behind her. She pulled on them to ensure they were tight enough. Satisfied, she turned her attention toward the laser.

She had seen it used once before but had never herself operated it. In fact, doing so would normally have been met with a high level of punishment, as she lacked the necessary clearance or training. As such, she had no clue how to even turn it on.

A row of buttons and switches lined the device's control panel. She studied them quickly, hoping to gain some insight into their functions from their nondescript colors and faded labels.

The pounding on the door grew louder by the moment.

Best guess, she thought. Ava flipped a switch on the far left of the panel which was a little larger than the rest. The device came to life with a pained but stable purr. *One for one.* She then moved to a set of three buttons to the right of the first switch. Red, black, and blue. *Red is bad? Blue is good? Black is...black? Or is black good?* Her hands shook as she decided on the right button to press.

The screams from the other side of the lab door had grown painfully loud, and each one matched the ever-increasing power of the impacts on the door. With a final cry from the attacking monstrosity, the door exploded off its hinges and came crashing to the ground some fifteen feet away.

"Black?" she asked aloud as she pressed the corresponding button. The machine squealed aggressively and began to vibrate unsteadily. "Okay okay, not black!" She pressed the black button again to calm the machine. "Blue then!" She hit the button and waited impatiently as the machine seemed to rev up, its sounds barely audible over the abomination beginning its trudge into the room towards her. It was slow at first, but it picked up speed with a terrifying veracity. Ava was running out of time.

She flipped a set of switches that she hoped were the final primers and aimed the laser at the monster as it arrived near the center of the lab. Its gait shifted and faltered with each step, likely caused by Ava's previous attack, but it wouldn't prevent it from taking one more victim. It screamed viciously at her.

The laser began what she hoped were its final series of startup processes, whirring and whining in progressively higher pitched tones and vibrations.

Her grip on the laser's handles tightened and her

thumb hovered anxiously over the trigger. She swallowed deep, hoping her plan would work. She fought the desire to undo her straps and run as the creature grew closer, almost within striking distance.

Suddenly, the laser's whine reached its peak and stopped abruptly. It was followed quickly by a surprisingly innocuous, almost playful beep.

With a ferocity matched only by the beast coming at her, Ava swung the laser away from the monster and hard to the left.

She had remembered something important about this room while deciding her plan of action back in the hallway. There wasn't just one way into or out of the survey lab. There were, in fact, two. The first was the door both Ava and the creature had entered through. The other was a massive hangar door, twenty feet wide and 15 feet tall, that ran along the large wall to Ava's left. It led directly out into space and was used when bringing in large samples. On a typical day, the door would only be accessible using a supervisor-provided access code and express clearance to open it. Today was not a typical day.

Ava aimed the laser at a set of buckles that ran alongside the right side of the bay door. She looked over at the beast, which reached out with a horrible cry, impatient to claim the final crew member of Somnambulist Station.

"No assimilation today, asshole."

She hit the bright red ignition trigger and the

laser threw a hot purple beam of radiation at the metal clamps. The rusted metal disintegrated immediately, and the laser cut a hole straight through to the outside.

At first, she could only hear a small hiss. Then cracks began to form away from the small hole and the door began to creak. Then the hiss became a quiet whoosh. Then a loud one. Ava tensed and grabbed the straps around her waist tight. The door made one final groan and then exploded outwards into space. The fast expulsion of air from the massive lab became a hurricane, pulling every loose object with it. The sound was painfully loud, but it was no match for the immense force that pulled on Ava. She could feel the straps tighten as they fought to hold her against the wall and she winced as they squeezed her insides sharply.

Even over the winds, she could hear the beast scream as it pawed at the world around it for some final lifeline. Its many fingers on its many hands reached out in all directions but there was nothing. With one last sad, horrid yell, it was sucked out into the abyss.

It felt as though it took forever, but eventually the last of the air left the lab and the winds stopped. The straps had held and, despite the intense pain in her abdomen, Ava was in one piece. She looked out of the now massive opening of the survey lab wall. The contents of the lab were moving fast in a large group away from the station. She could no longer recognize any individual object, but she knew the doctor's abomination was freezing and dying a horrible, painful death. For the first time since this had all started, she felt happy.

She stared down at Earth-Two, which was slowly growing brighter as the sun rose on the hemisphere facing the station. A group of approaching objects on the right side of the planet caught her attention. They twinkled brightly in the light of the Sun, but they became increasingly recognizable as they grew closer. It was the shuttles from the other stations.

Ava could feel tears escape her eyes. She didn't stop them. She welcomed the cold on her face.

She reached back and untied the straps, letting the artificial gravity of the station pull her body to the ground. It had been what felt like an eternity, but Ava finally closed her eyes. She let sleep take her with a smile on her face.

The Beginning of the Beginning of Us as We Know It

Well, this sucks.

The world is dusty and dirty and, quite frankly, pretty boring. There are trees and rocks and dirt and sand and just about jack shit else.

Wait, is that a bug?

Yeah, there's a bug over there I think, but still, mostly nothing.

Why did they choose this planet? Of all the places they could have chosen to exile me to, they chose Earth, this lonely rock out on the edge of space. Dicks.

I'm standing, but something feels wrong, like very wrong. I'm...short?

I hold my hands up and- oh boy am I pale. And

I'm fleshy. Why am I fleshy? And hairy. And dirty. Why is there so much dirt? They could have uploaded my mind into anything and they chose this lame, pale, dirty creature.

I can crouch and jump and stretch around. It's clumsy, but the limbs are flexible and provide a pretty good range of motion. Not as good as my original body, mind you, but what are you gonna do? Honestly, I feel bad for the poor schmuck whose body this was. I need it more now, sorry.

I have two arms and two legs, five fingers per hand and five toes per foot. At least they gave me something with opposable thumbs. Poor Ottofax got stuck in that sea slug. So at least this is better than that.

I pick up a rock and squeeze tight. Not bad. I throw it hard at a tree nearby and it hits with a thunk. A loud shriek cuts through the mostly silent surroundings and a two-winged creature bursts from the tree foliage and into the sky. What a weird place this is.

Are those hoppler fruits? I walk over to a bright red fruit hanging from one of the tree's low branches. There are a ton of them. I pick it. I open my mouth as wide as I possibly can and shove the whole bad boy in there. Ow! Okay- yeah no. Too big. I take it out but now it's covered in some sort of liquid. My whole mouth seems to be filled with it. A lubricant? Geez, now that I know it's there it's pretty gross.

I use the tiny, hard protrusions in my mouth to tear a smaller piece from the fruit. Sweet, juicy, but definitely no hoppler. It isn't an acaer bean either. Who knows? As long as it isn't poisonous or makes me explode, it's food. Ew- wait- it has some sort of seeds. I let the little black pits fall out of my mouth onto the dirt.

Time to find...something. I can hear rushing liquid, so I walk past the tree in the direction of the sound. It's coming from a stream of liquid dihydrogen monoxide. I had heard this stuff was prevalent on this planet, even necessary, but back home it was highly corrosive to our bodies. Here? Not so sure.

Across the stream from me, a large quadrupedal creature is bent down with its snout in the liquid. I guess it's safe for these carbon-based bodies. I follow suit and shove my head underneath the surface of the liquid. I breathe in hard. Note to self, horrible idea.

Okay, I've got the hang of it. Honestly, I feel pretty good now. My innards feel full and satisfied. I'm ready. Not sure for what, but I am.

I think it's about time to plan my inevitable revenge and the unflinchingly savage annihilation of those that trapped me here.

Do I deserve my imprisonment? Well...I mean, yeah. I almost certainly do. I did some horrific, messed up things. Does that mean I should deal with it and suffer until this body inevitably crumbles to dust? Nope. Screw that. Revenge sounds way more fun.

I follow the stream until I come across a pile of rocks that appears to have been grouped intentionally.

One of those creatures that had been nourishing itself at the stream lay dead and bloodied some distance from the rocks. Its outer fur is matted down and hardened from dried blood and mud. There is an opening to a large cave to my right and I can hear something moving around inside. My first recruit?

I walk into the dark cave. My new eyes adjust quickly and focus on a hunched over figure. It's using large stones to break smaller ones into sharper, smaller pieces. My presence shocks it, and it raises a stick with one of those sharpened rocks tied to the end of it. It's grunting aggressively, vocalizing with an assortment of meaningless sounds. Clearly, it's an idiot. This'll be harder than I assumed.

I raise my hands up in surrender, hoping it'll send a clear enough message. *I come in peace.*

It lowers its weapon and I walk further towards it. Even in the darkness of the damp cave, I can tell it's the same species as my new body. Its pale skin is covered in a thin layer of light, wispy hair, which becomes thick and wavy at the top of its head. It has a high, arched brow and wide, short nose that flares at me as I get closer.

I reach my hand out for the weapon but it swings it wildly in my direction. I'm out of the weapon's reach so it makes no contact. Maybe I'm coming on a little too strong. Time to take a step back. I leave the cave back out towards the dead, bloodied creature laying on the hard ground. I bend down next to the carcass and look around for some sort of apparent wound or opening. I find one and reach in with my hands. I grip and pull, tearing some red meat out.

I walk back into the cave and toss the scrap of meat towards the cowering and confused creature. I hope that the carcass serves as food and isn't instead some sort of ritual sacrifice or a dead friend.

The being eyes the meat, eyes me, eyes the meat, walks forward, grips the meat, and then takes a large bite out of the piece. Food...duly noted.

It then approaches me and I again reach my hand out for the weapon. It coos and grunts but tentatively places it into my hand.

Even across the universe, the quickest way to a new friend is through its stomach.

I back up and test the weapon, swinging it wide through the air. Heavier than I expected in my new, fragile arms but I can imagine it would be seemingly successful if put to good use. It has a pointy end. Good enough for me.

I bend down next to my new friend and motion towards another small pile of rocks. It looks at me confused, but after a few moments of grunts and coos, it crouch-walks its way over and falls flat on its bottom. I reach for a small pile of plant life lying on the hard stone floor and place it amongst the pile of rocks.

The fleshy idiot watches fascinated as I repeatedly scrape the weapon's tip against a flat stone. It only takes a few attempts before bright amber sparks start sputtering from the contact point on the stone. They fall hot against the dry plants.

Fire. It's universal, baby.

The creature panics immediately as the fire comes to life in front of it, as if it has never seen fire before.

It sticks its hand straight into the bright red flames.

Apparently, it hasn't seen fire before.

It howls with pain and crawls deep into the bowels of the cave. It whimpers. I chuckle. What are you gonna do? Everyone learns the hard way. I light the end of the weapon's handle ablaze and walk towards my cowering friend. The torch throws deep, intense shadows on the cave walls.

How do you communicate with an imbecile when you can't speak its language? Math? Science?

I stare at it for some time, watching as it glances from me, to the fire, back to me.

Pictures. You communicate with pictures.

I reach down and stick my fingers into a pile of wet mud.

The mud is cold against my new skin. I illuminate a flat section of stone wall next to me. My friend's beady, inset eyes follow the torch towards the wall. I drag the mud along the cold surface in swirling patterns, aggressive lines, and winding curves.

It's a sprawling canvas showing my original physical body, explaining my existence in this place and my goals for domination and revenge, and thoroughly detailing the involvement of my new friend and their people in those plans. I stand back to admire my completed artwork.

Damn, that sucks. Clearly my lack of talent transferred over.

The hodgepodge of shapes clearly has a different effect on my new friend. It's staring deeply, more deeply than I've ever seen anything stare at something. It reaches down into the mud, scoops up a small bit into its hand, and tentatively draws a small circle onto the wall.

It howls in victory and jumps fast and excited around its home.

I sigh with relief. Progress.

Let's get to work.

The Golden Spiral

I could hear the rain against the sheet metal roofing of the glorified shed that we called a lab. The air foreshadowed a coldness in the coming night. The low lighting within our small space created monstrous shadows which shifted and contorted under the swinging bulb.

The others had since left. I had told them to leave, to let me do this myself. This was more than just some job or hobby for all of us, but it was even more than that for me. It was a part of me. This system was as much me as I was me, and as such I needed to see it through alone.

The technology we had developed was highly advanced and was unceremoniously out of place in the dilapidated shed. The glimmering metal of the server racks stood out against the dull, rusting walls behind them.

My breath escaped my mouth and nose in bursts

and increasingly more frequent, more voluminous wisps of steam. I could feel my heart trying to escape my chest.

I stared down at the computer screen in front of me. My hands sat on the mechanical keyboard, but I struggled to bring them to motion. The flashing white cursor taunted me. I couldn't reconcile why I was so nervous. Maybe it was that, after so many thousands of hours of work, I was afraid the system wouldn't work. Maybe I was afraid it would.

We had developed one of the world's first truly-operational quantum computers. For reference, where an everyday personal computer could run hundreds of millions or sometimes billions of operations per second, our quantum computer could run trillions. It provided an increase in computing power that could allow processing of information on a scale never before seen.

We had decided to build the computer in what amounted to little more than a large backyard shed. Not to say we hadn't attempted for a more dignified setup, but it's hard to convince people to finance a group of mostly ostracized scientists with a pension for admittedly grandiose ideas.

The autonomy had its advantages though, in that we didn't have to make any concessions. It could be built and used the way we chose.

As such, we decided its first use should be a grand one. We'd try to answer one of humanity's greatest unanswered questions.

Where did we come from?

I typed a command into the computer and hit enter. A flurry of text scrolled down the terminal window with a veracity that was both frightening and exhilarating. A large window popped up after a few moments. It was a simulation of the Universe starting from time zero.

It was black. Nothing.

Then, with a click of the mouse, I hit play and watched as the blackness erupted with light. Thousands and then tens of thousands and then millions of years passed in the simulation as globules of matter began to come together, the fledgling galaxies and clusters of galaxies, each with millions of newborn stars. I sped up the process and "zoomed out" on the universe. The peripheral, empty space around the edges of the screen was progressively filled up with swirling colors and undulating masses.

I paused the simulation to check the data stream coming in. The simulation wasn't designed to be particularly accurate in terms of simulating the actual, real-life objects that exist in our own universe. Such a simulation was, in theory, impossible. This system was, instead, designed to reverse-engineer the origin of the cosmos based on what scientists today believed to be true of the virgin Universe.

The data seemed to be confirming the observable science better than we could have ever hoped. The size and density of the simulated universe was exactly what our theoretical and mathematical models predicted for the specific age at which I had paused it. I dragged the simulation around, viewing it from all angles, eyeing the beautiful web-like structures it had created. Satisfied, I moved it further forward in time.

Again, it expanded and blossomed and pushed farther into the void.

The city was quiet this time of the year. The cold crawled through the cracks in the walls and clung to me. I shivered in the loneliness I suddenly felt, staring at the magnificent, awesome synthesis of years of our work. It was hard not to feel strange at the dichotomy between the unquestionable level of potentially world-altering technology within this shed and the quaint, quiet city-bordering suburbia just outside.

I slowed the simulation as it neared the time around which our own solar system was born and paused it as it approximately reached our current epoch, around a few thousand years in the past. I checked the data once more. Again, it was exact, or as exact as it could be. The percentages of matter, dark matter, and dark energy all read almost identical to those predicted by the most advanced theories. The simulation by this point was infinite, as our own universe was believed to be.

It was working. It was confirmation that we had always been right, that the Big Bang was what we thought, that everything we know truly did come from an infinitely dense nothingness. The Universe really is an infinite expanse of every and potentially all possible things. It was only a simulation, but the feeling of smallness crept over me with an invasiveness that further increased the feeling of stark coldness in my insides.

One of the many benefits of an almost incomputable, unfathomably powerful computer was that it had a full grasp on all of the objects in the infinite simulation. Out of curiosity, I found myself filtering for objects like our Sun. A list appeared in a separate window with what I could only assume was an almost uncountable number of singular objects. I filtered further, this time for stars like our own with planets in orbit. Again, uncountable. Stars like our own with planets within the habitable zone. Infinite. I leaned back awestruck. I clicked through a few of the objects that appeared on the list and was each time zoomed through the simulation until the object came into view. They all looked mostly the same, the star's bright yellow-white bodies surrounded by a simulated planet here or there, sometimes more.

I found myself filtering further.

A star like our own.

Eight planets in orbit.

Each with the exact characteristics of our own eight planets.

I chuckled to myself as the key clacked under the pressure from my finger, expecting, even in the infinite cosmos of the simulation, for it to return nothing. The system thought momentarily and then completed its search. Rather than returning nothing, it returned a single result. A single, identical, eight-planet system to our own.

Impossible.

This simulation was supposed to create a random universe, a fictional cosmos bounded by real physics. Yet, it had somehow predicted our solar system exactly. The reverberations of the rain against the roof seemed louder, more overbearing than normal. I felt cold and lost.

The curiosity gnawed at me. I considered not exploring further, not viewing the system up close, not answering any of my million questions. Although, really, what was the danger in exploring further? What harm could a computer simulation really cause? I swallowed my trepidation and continued on.

I selected the system and watched as the simulation zoomed past billowing swirls of light and dust until it stopped hard and fast, centered on the Sun. Around it orbited eight planets, and far beyond them, forming a perforated outer boundary to the solar system, circled a giant spherical shell of small rocky bodies, the Oort Cloud. It *was* our solar system. It looked identical to every model I had ever seen of it.

Without considering the implications, I zoomed in on Earth. *Wait*, I thought suddenly as it appeared larger on my screen. It was different. It was green and blue and shining in the void, but something was wrong. The land masses were wrong; they were not where they should have been. Instead of multiple large masses spread across the globe, it was a single, irregular, gigantic continent. I spun it around and changed my angle of viewing and I finally recognized what I was seeing.

Pangea. The supercontinent that existed during the time of the early dinosaurs. To confirm my suspicions, I searched the web for a picture of Pangea, for what scientists believed it had looked like. It was almost exact. *You've got to be kidding me.* I couldn't help but chuckle in disbelief.

I pushed the simulation forward in time, first a few years, then hundreds and thousands and then millions passed. Pangea shifted and cracked and then was pulled apart by some invisible force. 200 million years ago, 150, 100...

I watched in awed horror as an asteroid dozens of miles in diameter careened out from the void towards Earth. I was helpless as it collided with the surface, throwing up walls of red, glowing mantle. The planet was swallowed by a sea of death, a cloud of dark embers.

I sped forward as the dark orange gave way to a bright white, an ice age.

Farther forward. The planet spun, the seasons changed across its surface. The clock in the upper right corner of the screen displayed a measure of the years back from the present. -100,000, -50,000. -10,000. I stared with painfully dry eyes as the clock ticked closer down to 0. I slowed it as I began to notice a difference in the dark side of the planet.

Tiny sparkles of light began to appear amongst the coasts of the United States and Europe. Then more and then finally they speckled much of the world's land masses. I was suddenly overwhelmed by an abject, unflinching nausea.

This simulation hadn't just perfectly simulated the objects of our solar system. It hadn't just perfectly simulated our planet, our planet's history. It had somehow, in some way entirely incomprehensible to me, predicted and simulated *us*. I was actively watching a perfect simulation of the human species.

We hadn't just created a computer capable of creating a realistic, *analogous* universe, we had created a computer that simulated *the* Universe.

I couldn't tell if I was happy or horrified.

I checked the clock in the simulation. -51. It was now 1968. Which meant...

I spun the simulation around so that it was focused on the east-central coast of Florida. I slowly pushed the time forward.

I kept my view of the planet at a distance. I wasn't sure how powerful the simulation's rendering capabilities truly were. Could I pull all the way in and actually watch? Would I be able to see the individuals, see life brimming across the surface? The thought made me shudder.

Instead, I focused my attention on the clock. -49.78 years back from the present. July 16, 1969. First there was nothing. At this distance, in the bright sun of the summer day, there was nothing beyond the spotted Floridian coastline. I strained my eyes on a particular location, hoping to pick it out amongst the deep greens and blues that surrounded it. After a few minutes, a thin, almost entirely unnoticeable line—a stream of puffy grey smoke—began to appear perpendicular to the surface. As it extended away from the land, slowly at first, it picked up speed. I smiled as I noticed a sparkle atop the pillar of smoke. The grey line trailing the space shuttle eventually subsided and I lost sight of it as it exited the Earth's thin atmosphere, but I knew it was there, rocketing its way towards the Moon.

I leaned back in my worn leather chair. It squeaked lightly as its plastic and metal base strained under the shifting weight. I thought maybe the rain had subsided, because I could no longer hear it. A quick look out the small window to my right confirmed the rain was just as heavy, just as persistent as it was before. The singular sound I could hear, the sound of my heart beating, was loud in my ears.

The simulation ran forward. I sat there staring mindlessly, but I realized after some time that it had almost caught up to the present. I paused it just before it did.

Would it keep going? It was an exciting, albeit slightly scary, thought, but it had been entirely accurate up to this point. Could it show me the future? I had lost sight of what I was dealing with. Was it only a simulation? How could it just be a simulation? How could it just be the system's "best guess"?

I couldn't. How could I live knowing? No one had the right to know what came next. No human should have that knowledge. Humanity is motivated by a lack of knowledge of the future, isn't it? But then, we had surpassed that hadn't we? In creating this system, we had risen above that lowly level of humankind.

I hit play and watched in silence as the clock turned from the negatives to the positives.

I didn't stop it as it moved further. +1 year, +2, +10. I watched as the yellow sparkling lights in the darkness doubled, tripled, multiplied and then grew higher into the skies, higher and denser until it was no longer yellow and white lights, but lights of all colors. They were brighter, more luminescent, more omniscient in the darkness. Their control of the surface was unending, and their seemingly random twinkle made them appear almost sentient.

+75. +80.

Then the lights went out. The planet went dark. I slowed the progression to a real-time crawl. I reversed back to the moment of blackout. +91. All at once, the world's lights blinked out.

What could have caused a world-wide power loss? I sped up the clock and watched intently. The darkness remained for some time. Then, quick bursts of light sprung out around the planet's surface. It wasn't an electrically powered light, no. I feared pulling closer and inherently strained to determine the cause. The bursts became more frequent, larger, more intrusive.

War.

Then, again, nothing. The planet fell all but entirely silent.

The days, weeks, ticked by.

The northern hemisphere erupted into light. I had been straining my eyes so hard for any sign of life that the brightness shocked me, hurting my retinas. I flinched and leaned back in pain, rubbing my hands deep against my eyelids in the hopes it would dull the pain and push the tears away. I regained some level of sight, but it still took a few moments to register what had happened. I spun the time back to watch it again and readied myself against the brightness.

First one, then two, then more, maybe a dozen massive bursts of harsh orange rippled across Asia. Mushroom clouds lifted high into the atmosphere with each one. The clouds dispersed as they hit the ceiling of the world and spread across the planet in massive swathes. Beneath the thick, black atmosphere, more of the bursts could be seen erupting from the other side of the planet. I swung around the Earth to confirm as much as new plumes filled the skies.

My skin was hot and prickled as blood rose to the surface. The pressure in my head felt as though it could push my eyeballs onto the floor. My throat was tight and dry and seemed ready to swallow itself.

I let the simulation continue as I fell backwards

into my chair once again, but it didn't matter. There was nothing left. Just blackness, dark and endless clouds forming a deathly cage around a once vibrant planet.

The universe could take me then and there and I wouldn't have argued. The regret and shame and cognizance wrapped itself around my cold, stilted frame.

After some time, I stood up slowly and stepped back away from the screen. I walked around the stack of servers along one of the shed's walls and pulled the main power cable from the massive power supply. The system powered down with a high-pitched electrical whir and the dive bombing sound of detuned digital noise.

My legs suddenly grew weak and I fell uneasily to the ground, catching myself with my hands as my backside reached the hard concrete. What I had seen couldn't have been real. It had to have been just a guess, an educated guess based on...I don't know what. No matter how horrifyingly accurate the simulation was in somehow predicting and simulating the past, the future could only ever be an assumption, right?

The cold permeated from the floor through my pants and up my hands and forearms. I stood, brushing the dirt from my hands and pants.

It's not real. I don't know how, but I managed to convince myself of that. A feeling of calm swept over me. In a way, the idea that I was crazy or hallucinating or simply that the simulation was somehow *wrong* was more comforting to me than the idea that what I had just seen had been entirely real, that I had just witnessed a true prediction of the world's doom.

I pulled on my jacket, walked towards the door, paused as I looked back toward the mountains of tech inside and the lonely console in the center, and walked out the door. I'm not sure where I was going, or what I hoped to find there, but I shut the light off and let the door close hard behind me.

The rain was still falling hard. I was soaked in seconds, but it felt nice. Each drop was a needle against my skin, injecting me with a sense of awareness, of awakening, that I hadn't had before. I stood there and let it fall over me.

But then I wasn't there. I suddenly found myself plugging the server rack back in. My body was running on autopilot. I couldn't tell if I was controlling my own self or it was something else entirely. Maybe the rain had awakened a curiosity that I had assumed or hoped I had killed minutes before.

A loud buzz and a digital purr accompanied the quantum computer as it powered back on. As if controlled by some vindictive puppet master, I sat back down at the console.

I typed in the current date with cold, autonomous fingers and watched as the simulation zoomed and shifted and changed. I filtered once more for our solar system. Again, the colors expanded and appeared and disappeared across the screen as the simulation flew to the destination. I pulled in close to Earth. I tried to stop myself, but I couldn't. My willpower seemed to weaken the more I tried.

I needed to know.

I typed in a set of longitude and latitude coordinates. The planet spun until it was focused on the location from orbit. I zoomed into the planet fast, the blue and green and whites now expanding huge on the screen. I entered the atmosphere, I passed through a thick layer of clouds, a heavy storm. The view was quickly filled with tall buildings and bright lights. Closer, further, until I paused the simulation as it was 100 feet above the ground. A small-ish, shabby-looking metal building sat directly in the center of the view. Even in the darkness of night, it was an unmistakable object.

I moved the simulation closer, slowly, until it was only five or six feet above the grass floor. With a slow, shaky hand, I dragged the viewing angle up, until it was aimed directly into the doorway of the structure.

Sitting inside at the center console, disheveled and wet, was me.

I raised my right arm and watched in horror as my simulation doppelgänger did the same.

Sols of Our Lives

"The fuck?" Laszki snorted. "This is a joke, right? Has to be."

"That's one really expensive joke," Emily responded coldly. The thin breeze pushed a light layer of rust-colored dust onto her visor. She wiped it away mindlessly with her glove.

"I mean come on, Commander...someone's messing with us. They fly it up here with one of the resourcing missions maybe?" he questioned. Emily tapped again at the small screen on her wrist. They stood directly on the small dot as it pinged rhythmically on her GPS.

"But how'd they get it all the way out here? We're easily a few klicks from the dome. The order came right from the top of the food chain. Unknown signal," Emily said back. "That's a lot of work to go through to mess with us. I mean we honestly have way more important things to be doing." Laszki shrugged and nodded, the look on his face as twisted in confusion as hers. They were both afraid to touch it. "We're the first ones on this planet. Who would have put this here?"

As if the first manned mission to Mars wasn't eventful enough, Laszki and Emily stood dumbfounded, staring at a small black box. It was maybe a foot in all dimensions and black as night. Definitely not natural.

"Well someone did," he said back after a short pause. "It's certainly no Martian rock. We tell the team, right?" She could feel him looking over at her, but at that moment, she was entirely unsure of what to do. "Emily?"

"We tell the team, yeah. Radio it in. Have them meet us in the dome." She could see him tap away at his wrist from the corner of her visor, presumably to open a wideband comm channel.

"Guys...we've, uh, got something. I don't know what, but we've got something. The Commander wants you all home. We'll be back soon."

Emily walked forward slowly in the low Martian gravity. The box sat on a perfectly flat patch of dirt, void of any rock or sediment larger than an Earthly grain of sand. She bent down as gracefully as her suit would allow, swallowed deep, and grabbed it. Nothing. No spontaneous combustion, no sudden evaporation. It was just a smooth black box.

"We're good, I think. Let's go." She crawled into the large-minivan-sized rover cautiously, placing the object on a small mat underneath the sample bench. Laszki hit the accelerator, and, as the sudden motion pushed her back in her seat, she hoped they had made the right decision.

What do I say? This has to be fake, or a joke, or something, Emily thought. *There has to be something, just something that could explain it. Twenty-one sols into the first manned mission to the Red Planet with no issue, and then this. I suppose exploration into the unknown is the whole point, right?*

They pulled up to the dome, their home away from home for three months. The once white and now slightly reddish semi-sphere sat in stark contrast to the burnt red landscape. Laszki and Emily disembarked from the rover and entered the dome's airlock. Emily grasped the object tight. The perspiration from her hands was starting to gather in her thick gloves. A green light and a tri-tone beep signaled the space had reached one atmosphere in pressure and they proceeded through the second airlock door.

Four pairs of confused eyes fell upon the two as they made their way into the large, mostly open common room of the dome. It only took a short time for their gaze to fall upon the shocking object in Emily's hands.

"Little help?" Laszki said impatiently, gesturing towards himself and then to her. It was enough to break the stares, and two of the four went to work helping them out of their EVA suits. Emily was careful to place the object on the center table before they got too far, but she never took her eyes off of it. Nothing had changed since she'd first picked it up, but the nervous feeling crawling up her spine had only gotten worse.

"What is it?" Mark, the mission's geologist and mechanical engineer, asked as we circled the table.

"You guys just found it out there? This was the signal that Homebase wanted you to look at?" Cochran, the mission's pilot and physicist. "I just assumed it was one of the mining drones going off-script or something. I didn't expect...whatever the hell this is." His thick Glasgow accent accentuated the confusion in his voice.

"It was just sort of there. The signal itself was just a locational radio ping. Vague, but nothing unusual," Emily responded. "It was like it wanted us to find it..."

"*It* wanted you to find it? It's a fucking box, Emily. *It* doesn't want anything. Someone put it there! Someone had to have put it there." The crew's medical officer, Bai. "Have you guys reported it? Down to Homebase I mean?" she asked. Laszki looked over at Emily nervously with the completion of Bai's question. She considered it for a few moments but eventually returned his look with a nod.

"We...we don't know if we should," he said, looking at the box while avoiding everyone's gaze. The consensus was clear on Laszki's comment, but the eyes in the room fell upon Emily.

"What do you mean "don't know if we

should"? We just found a damn box, clearly not natural, sitting on the surface of Mars," Bai said with frustration that she made no attempt to hide. "Oh, and *it* apparently called *us*. I think, if there was ever anything we absolutely *should* contact Homebase about, it's this!" Emily looked at Bai sharply, who glared back. Cochran looked surprised at the tone she was using with the commanding officer of their mission.

"Can't we just bring it back out there? Put it back where it came from and forget about it? Or maybe let's destroy it. It's not an issue if it doesn't exist." Cochran had a gruff sincerity that Emily and her crew appreciated, even if it was sometimes a little brash, but it was clear in his voice that even he knew his suggestions weren't the right call.

"This isn't that simple you guys," Emily said sternly, aimed at no one in particular. "We can all agree that we don't know what this thing is or what it do-"

"Well, we can try to find out, no?" Anna, the mission's botanist and primary dome engineer, said, speaking for the first time. "You touched it with your gloved hands, Commander, but none of us have touched it unprotected. A simple experiment. Worth a shot?"

"We have no clue what this thing's gonna do," Laszki said, but Emily knew this was the inevitable, and smart, option, even if it may have been a little risky. They could spend time running tests from afar, or leave it untouched entirely, but Mission Control would inevitably want them to do *something*. And even Emily knew it was best they skip the bureaucracy.

"She's right," Emily said, more calmly than she had anticipated. "I'll do it. It's my mission...my responsibility." Her five crew members all nodded in agreement as they stepped back a few paces.

She reached out slowly and touched the top lightly with the tips of her fingers. When nothing happened after a few seconds, she placed her palm flat against the smooth surface. The material was strange. Despite sitting out in the cold Martian air for who knows how long, it felt as though it had matched the temperature of the room in only a few short minutes. And the color was *dark*. Much darker than it had appeared out in the copper sunlight. Light seemed to truly disappear inside of it. No reflection, no glares or glints under the harsh white light of the dome. Just darkness. She picked her hand up and touched it again, this time on the side. Nothing seemed to change.

"I have to be honest, I'm not sure what I expected, but I at least expected something. I mean, maybe it's just, I don't know, a black bo-" Cochran's sentence was stopped short. A faint, thin ring of blue light had suddenly appeared on the top of the box. Its glow increased slowly, and then quickly until it began throwing visible light on the mostly neutral colored clothing of the six astronauts standing around it.

"Uh, progress?" Laszki said anxiously. The diffuse light emanating from the box began to change again, focusing into a small-ish area a few inches above the box itself, like a hologram. The color swirled in a blue mist, until, before their shocked eyes, it formed words.

"Oh boy. I shouldn't have eaten that freeze-dried burrito...that's Space 101...you don't eat the freeze-dried burritos," Mark mumbled.

"Nope, we're seeing it too, buddy," replied Cochran.

"What the fuck?"

"Holy crap."

"Damn."

"I don't get it," said Bai amongst the statements of shock and confusion, although she knew no one else understood it either.

"*Reset*. What does it mean by *reset*?" Emily asked. The message that had materialized above the box was clear as day. The letters were crisp and unmistakable.

Congratulations. Your species has once again achieved interplanetary travel. Enjoy the pride you must all feel, for you will soon be reset.

"Why is it in Russian?" Anna asked.

"You're seeing it in Russian?" Mark asked, surprised. "Looks like English to me."

"I'm seeing it in Chinese!" Bai shouted.

"Fuckin' cool," Cochran said with a chuckle of disbelief.

"Alright, so it's displaying the message in each of our native languages," Emily said. "Not sure how that works, but okay. So, it knows us somehow, or is, I don't know, learning about us." *What am I even saying anymore? What is happening?* she thought to herself. As the moments went on, Emily found the process of keeping the wall up between the very confused, horrified, anxious thoughts and the mostly calm words that were exiting her mouth to be incredibly difficult. She'd flown on a dozen space missions, studied real, hard science her entire adult life, but this was magic to her. There was nothing in her head to explain this away.

"We have to tell Earth," Bai interjected.

"What do we say, Bai?" Laszki asked. "'Hey guys, what's up? Oh yeah, we're doing pretty good, except we found a box in the middle of a damn Martian desert and it's talking to us and, oh yeah, it says it's going to reset us, whatever the hell that means.'" Bai huffed and walked back from the table. Laszki's response had clearly gotten under her skin. Cochran reached out and put a hand on her shoulder before speaking to the rest of us.

"She's right," he said. "If it was up to me, I'd toss it back out where it came from, bury it a hundred meters down, and pretend none of this ever happened, but it's not up to me and...I mean, for God's sake...they might at least be able to tell us what to do."

"Yeah, that...or the message, with our luck, will get intercepted on the way down. You'll have religious cults committing mass suicide by dinnertime," Laszki commented back with a bite that likely hit harder than he intended.

"Laszki, we're just eyes and ears up here. They need to know," Emily conceded. She stopped for a minute, deciding whether or not her next decision was the right one. The fate of this mission was on her, and she knew it, but now it felt like the fate of something far larger was, too.

"Commander...Emily...what do we do?" Laszki's words were sincere, and the yearning for an answer was deeply palpable. Emily swallowed hard and followed it with a slow, deep breath.

"Open a channel to Homebase."

Bai had been eagerly waiting for her to say just that. She had been standing at the ready over the comms terminal. "Yes, Commander."

All this time, the message had remained floating above its home. Emily stood staring at it, wondering how in God's name she would explain it to Mission Control. She couldn't help the feeling that Homebase would think they'd gone mad. Space sickness or something. They'd scrap the mission and bring the crew home. Both them and the box would be studied, locked in some room somewhere for the rest of their lives. She knew how the government worked, she knew the dark secrets they kept, and, if this was what everything they were experiencing implied it was, they'd become one of those dark secrets, too. Or at least that's what she thought, even if she knew the thought was perhaps slightly over-dramatic.

"Commander?" Bai's urgent tone pulled Emily's focus away from her worries. "We've got a problem."

"What is it, Bai?"

"We have no signal."

"Oh, you've got to be shitting me!" Cochran exclaimed with a frustrated flailing of his arms up into the air.

"What do you mean we have no sig-"

There was a knock at the airlock door.

The *inner* airlock door.

They all froze.

"Alright...and you guys heard that right?"

"Wasn't the burritos, Mark," Cochran murmured back.

It was clear as day. Not natural. No machine acting up. Just a knock at the door.

"The new neighbors maybe." Cochran was shushed by the others around him.

Emily walked towards the door slowly.

"Commander..." Laszki whispered nervously, shaking his head in disapproval.

"What the hell else are we supposed to do?" She growled back. "You want to hide? This place is not that big. I check it out now or it checks us out later. I vote now." She stared back at everyone expectantly. The lack of any clear responses seemed like as much of an *I agree* as she was going to get.

The five remaining astronauts crouched to the

floor. It was unnecessary, but it was the only instinctual response they could all agree on.

Something struck Emily as odd during her slow walk towards the door. They had yet to receive an outer door lock warning inside the dome. Its purpose was to alert the crew that the outer airlock door had not been closed or locked properly after a set time. But it never went off. Which meant the airlock had correctly pressurized. Which meant that the inner door was now unlocked. Which meant that whatever was waiting for them on the other side was consciously waiting for them when it very well could have just walked right in.

Emily's hands were shaking violently. She was cognizant of how uncharacteristic the nerves were for her, but she chalked it up to *what the fuck is going on*.

She grabbed the inner lever, swung it wide and then pulled the latch. The door swung open.

Emily was staring at a...person? No, it wasn't a person, although it was certainly shaped like one. Its matte-grey metal body stood almost perfectly still. Its face, or the area where a face would normally be, was a material like fogged glass. An undulating mass of small-ish yellow spheres, like neon ball bearings, could be seen in its otherwise hollow head behind the glassy faceplate.

"Hello," greeted a computerized voice. "It's nice to meet you, Commander Emily Darrow."

"Uh, hi."

"I see you've found it," it said, gesturing with one of its metallic arms towards the black box on the table. "We decided we'd wait to introduce ourselves until you had seen it, so as not to shock you."

"Shock us? You're fuckin' late to that party, mate," Cochran blurted out as he rose quickly from the crouched astronaut huddle and moved aggressively towards where Emily stood at the airlock. She shot him a look for the outburst and held up her hand to signal he stop speaking or else deal with her. He did with a huff.

"This thing is yours?" she asked the visitor.

"Oh, no. It is not. Quite the opposite. I've come to try to spare you the fate implied in its message, in the hopes that you can help us."

"Awesome. Well, sure, cool. Thanks for, uh, that." *Come on, Emily. Try at least a little harder to not sound like you're on a bad first date*, she thought resentfully to herself.

"I fear you must all be quite confused right now," said the alien machine creature to a room full of shocked eyes and jaws on the floor. "Myself and my people are part of a conglomerate of races, all working towards one common goal. Something your race is quite accustomed to: resistance."

It was clear to Emily at this point in the day that her reserves of incredulity and disbelief had run dry. It was hard, in the face of something so ridiculous, to not just give in and say *okay, I guess this is my life now.*

Her crew mates had moved farther forward into the room, closer to the airlock. Laszki stood to the side nervously, with his arms folded in some sort of timid act of self-defense. Cochran stood directly to the right of Emily with his chest puffed and his back straight, ready to pounce. Bai stood on the other side with less aggression than her Scottish crew mate but a more defined look of confusion than the others, her brow furrowed hard on her small face. She held a wrench tight in her left hand and her forearm muscles twitched with readiness. No one would have been surprised if she was the first to attack.

Mark stood back a few feet, not so much out of fear or nerves, but more out of an aloofness to the situation. Disbelief could be a powerful paralytic to the right person.

Anna appeared to Bai's left and started speaking. "Resistance? I do not know about the rest of you, but that word does not make me feel, what is the saying? Warm and fuzzy?" A harsh sound came from the creature that I could only assume was laughter.

"Can you please tell us, just, I don't know, anything?" Emily asked.

"Certainly. There is much to tell you."

"Okay, yeah. Do you want to come in?" *Look at you Emily, you're inviting an alien in for tea.*

"I'm going to have to ask you to come with me, actually." Its tone was continually polite, but that had felt like a command rather than a request.

"I'm gonna have to say hold up a minute there. We don't know who or what you are." Cochran's posture grew continually more combative as the moments went on. His wide body moved further towards the door. Even Cochran wasn't sure what would happen if he rushed the creature, but Emily wasn't interested in starting a war with it this early in their new relationship. She placed her arm across Cochran's chest.

"My big friend is right. We can't just abandon our mission like this," she said sincerely. "There are billions of people on our planet who know we are up here. It's likely at least a few of them would get a little worried if we suddenly stopped phoning home. You need to give us more than that."

"Very well, I owe you that much. As I said, my species is one of many who are standing up in resistance to another, far more virulent kind. They have many names, but for now, you can call them The Abyss. They're a relentless tidal wave, convinced of their superiority and who stop at nothing to keep all other species below them."

"What do you mean 'below them'?" Anna asked, confused at the specificity.

"To them, maintaining their supposed superiority is equivalent to a religious calling. It is the closest they can be to their god."

"Well how could they possibly ensure something like that?" Laszki asked.

"They developed a technology long ago, or perhaps found it—no one is truly sure of the history— that allows them to, let's say, *interact* with time. It serves two functions for those that control it. The first is that they can see certain events—important, catastrophic, what have you—for each new species that they come across. The second, and perhaps most horrible of its uses, is that it allows them to, essentially, reset time."

"Oh. That's...bad." Laszki said in response to his question's answer, glancing over at the now far-more-horrifying box on the table.

"How could anyone possibly know that they even do that if time is being fundamentally reset?" Emily asked curtly, sure that she had found a loophole in the creature's story.

"That, Commander, is why I said *essentially*. They aren't literally resetting time, per se. It's a bit complicated to explain, unfortunately." It paused for a moment to formulate an explanation for the expectant group in front of it. "First, they designate reset points for each new species. This is usually a point in time where the race is new, naive, and virgin within the universe...weak. They let the species evolve how it will through time, until it reaches The Point of No Return —the pivotal moment that each species becomes a danger to The Abyss's power. It is different for all species...for you, it is interplanetary travel...for others, perhaps the development of stone tools or the discovery of alien life. It is at that point that The Abyss uses their technology for its true purpose. A new timeline is created, branching from your original reset point, that time at which you were only just beginning. They merge the differences in that new timeline—only those specific solely to your species—back into this main one, essentially resetting your race. No species has ever passed their Point of No Return."

"Well that would surely affect the rest of the universe would it not?" Bai interjected loudly. "They can't just fake universal progression. We would be able to tell somehow! Right?"

"An understandable thought, but that is where you are wrong. There is, in fact, a great deal of faking going on. And it has not gone unnoticed or unfelt. Each reset sends deep ripples throughout the universe. It's pulling at the seams and there is little slack left."

"Holy shit, man. That's...a lot...to take in."

"Mark is right," Emily said, the exhaustion now audible in her voice. "Why are you here? Why are you telling us? Actually, why would they tell us?" She questioned while gesturing back at the floating message above the box.

Congratulations. Your species has once again achieved interplanetary travel. Enjoy the pride you must all feel, for you will soon be reset.

"If they are just going to reset us, why tell us at all?" she asked again.

The creature sighed, or at least that's what the astronauts thought it did, and it turned its head, aiming it slowly towards each member of the crew. It appeared to ponder its response before speaking once more.

"They are a sadistic race," it said slowly. "To

them, we are playthings to be toyed with. Why not have fun and meet your religious calling at the same time?" Emily shivered in the thought of the countless planets, races, and people cruelly dragged throughout their history. Over and over and over again. It wasn't just the bad things being reset each time. It was all good, too. All the happiness, all the triumphs, the relationships, the memories. All lost, and for what?

"That's fucked up," Laszki said solemnly.

"And that is why they don't kill us instead, isn't it?" Anna asked. A sudden tone of understanding appeared in her voice. "They would rather make us suffer. Whether we know it's happening or not, it's still horrible. They are erasing everything that we are, everything that we may have become."

The room was quiet. The creature stared at them.

"And you want us to come with you?" Bai asked.

"Yes."

"Why? And why would we ever agree?"

"We were hoping we could bring an end to their rewriting of time. The past should stay in the past, and it should only ever happen once. We will be the first to write a new chapter in the cosmos."

"But why us?"

"In all of this, my new friends, you have not thought to ask an obvious question." The creature looked at the astronauts stoically. The light flooded through the outer airlock window and bathed its metallic frame in tones of red and orange. Emily couldn't help but chuckle. Compared to the almost religious-looking scene in front of them, they must have looked like a pack of dull, antiquated idiots. She wondered, though, *what question does it mean? I have a million, but who's to say what's obvious and what's not.* As if on cue, it continued.

"If The Abyss can reset time, why not simply reset us all back to before we met, before our little conglomerate and its resistance began to take form within the galaxy? Why not change history once more, rip it apart and fit the puzzle pieces back together, keeping us controlled and at bay as they always have?" It paused, likely for dramatic effect. Cliché or not, it worked. The crew stared at it like children, stunned and silent in anticipation. "It's because of you. In meeting you, my species has passed its Point of No Return. For the first time, *we* have the advantage. And for the first time, we know exactly where they are. We're taking the fight to them."

"I'm in."

We turned wide-eyed towards Laszki, who was actively putting on his EVA suit. Emily was speechless, her mouth dry and hands shaking, but she was most surprised at Laszki's sudden courage.

He spoke again. "I mean what else are we going to do, right? I've had a good life. I've probably had a ton of them, actually, but I think I can spare one to do this."

His voice was shaky but strong.

Anna was next, nodding and grabbing her helmet off of the floor near the airlock door. She looked at Bai, who, despite the fear in her eyes, nodded as well.

"Heck it, I'm in, too," Mark said, pulling the EVA body sleeve he had draped around his chest up onto his shoulders. "This is all so weird and awful and awesome, so yeah, why not?"

Emily looked over at Cochran who was staring hard back at her. He looked at his crew mates, at the alien standing in the doorway, and back at his Commander.

"Eh, why the fuck not."

Emily sighed deep. Not a sad sigh or a frustrated sigh. A sigh of acknowledgment, of preparation. They were leaving behind their lives, everything, to join a war they had only just learned about, from a real, actual alien they only just met. To think that only this morning she was vacuum sealing her poop for fertilizer. Oh, how far they'd come.

"Alright," she said, zipping up her inner sleeve. "I guess...take us to your leader?"

Aurora

The rushing water comes up to just below my ankles. It's cold, but, despite the feeling of a light pressure pushing against my legs, I'm mostly numb to its presence. I try to see through the thick line of trees on either side of the river, but it's infinite. How long have I been standing here? A minute? Maybe twenty? I finally bring myself to motion, although it feels involuntary, with no sense of purpose or direction. Just motion.

The sound of the rushing river catches my attention the moment that I begin to move. Except, it's not the river, is it? It's of a lower register, one of those sounds you can feel in your insides, like a deep mechanical hum or a subwoofer at a rock concert. It's coming from everywhere, and turning my head as I move doesn't make a difference in the strength or directionality of the sound.

I wade against the current, slowly and surely towards what I can only guess is the horizon. The river

and lines of trees to my left and right appear to end
sharply against a blue-white sky that meets the horizon.
The hum grows louder, more persistent, as I move
towards the horizon; the sound seems to emanate from
everywhere—the trees, the water, myself.

No matter how hard I try to walk towards the
sky, it doesn't appear to grow any closer, and after some
time I stop altogether. I can't see the point in continuing
if I'm not getting any closer. Perhaps the tree line can
offer some rest.

The sound becomes harsh and immense as I turn
towards the shore. The white sky grows bright and
painful. I spin around looking for solace, for some
escape from the momentous throbbing in my head. Just
beyond the end of the river, sitting only slightly above
the horizon line is an immense, shifting mass. A shadow
made real. Just as soon as I recognize its existence, the
world explodes in a white light, and I am nowhere.

The rushing water comes up to just below my
knees. It pushes past me as if I'm not even here,
seemingly unaffected by the space I occupy. The trees
sway slightly in the warm, comfortable breeze. The hair
on the back of my neck rises from my sweating skin. Am
I being watched? The feeling increases as I move against
the current towards the horizon. I stop and scan the trees
but see nothing beyond shifting shadows amongst the
army of bright green conifers that flank me on either
side. Any number of animals likely live in these woods. I

push the paranoia aside in favor of a renewed focus.

I continue back towards the horizon, but as I push closer it seems to shift. It moves near, then farther away; it appears to expand in size and then shrink just as fast. I rub my eyes and the effect fades. Maybe I'm stressed, or maybe it's a byproduct of the bright sun reflecting off the sparkling water. Maybe I need some sleep.

Suddenly, I recognize something that's been here the whole time, something that I was ignoring, or maybe I've just been telling myself it wasn't real, that it's inside my head. A low hum permeates the air and seems to grow louder by the second. The sun expands and becomes endlessly bright in the sky, and then, nothing.

The blue sky is filled with color today as I stand in a large clearing, empty besides a thick layer of lush, bright green grass. Ribbons of blues and greens and reds and more billow against the azure backdrop. The sun feels larger and brighter than I remember, yet it's outshone by the aurora around it.

I can't help but feel awestruck, yet there's a nagging feeling, a sense that I don't belong here. Something's trying to pull me away. I continue to stare up at the sky despite the pressure inside of me to move. It reminds me of a vast undulating ocean, one perpetually just out of reach.

The blue of the sky grows white, and it begins to outshine the colors that swirl within it. An incredible hum erupts from all around me, loud in both my body and mind, and it too seems to tug on me. It grows exponentially loud as the seconds pass, and then the world erupts into light.

The rushing water comes up to just below my hips.

The skin on my neck begins to stiffen. A tingling sensation spreads along my back. I assume it's because of the cold water, but it's a feeling more akin to that of being watched or having your name called in a crowd. I know that no one has called me, but the feeling is just the same. No one stands along the tree line or further into the forest. I refocus my eyes for distance and peer behind me along the river. Now I see it.

Looming in the distance and standing atop the foamy water is a dark, smoking figure. Not human but not entirely inhuman, it stands and, as far as I can tell, stares back at me. It doesn't move and neither do I.

"Hello?" I call out uneasily, to no answer. "Who are you? Why are you here?" Nothing.

I take a small step in the direction of the figure. Its shadowy mass flies towards me the moment my body lurches forward. An angry, ghostly apparition. It comes at me faster than I could have possibly prepared for. I try to turn and run, but I'm slowed by the rushing water, holding me back like chains tied around my ankles. With a yell and a flailing of arms up to my face, the giant shadow collides with me and all I see is black.

The rushing water comes up to just below my elbows. The sound of the breeze through the trees, rustling the branches of the browning pines, is paralytic. I feel frozen standing in the cold water, but I know I have to move. The urge to suddenly run from this place is inescapable, but I know it's not that simple. This place, this river...it's a prison. No bars, no shackles, but I still feel trapped. I'm being sentenced to something, funneled along from one place to the next with no choice of my own.

Despite the flow of the current away from it, I'm drawn towards the horizon, the place where the river and trees seem to end and the sky takes over. I push towards it against the suggestion of the water.

A hum is birthed from the world around me as I get closer, louder and louder, shaking me to my core. The sky begins to glow with sparkling, twisting ribbons of color. They reach out to me against the increasingly bright light of the looming sun.

I can feel eyes against my back, but when I turn there is nothing. I turn back towards my goal, though, and am startled to see a massive shadow floating just above the edge where the river ends. I am terrified, yet I keep walking, fighting against the increasingly strong current that's pushing back against me with all it has.

The bright light and loud hum grow more powerful, and a surging pressure begins to develop inside of me. Every one of my atoms vibrates excitedly, and I feel like I'm about to burst. I can't help but stare up at the figure, which comes more into focus as I move close. It's human, but not. Not entirely recognizable, but familiar. Like something once removed from a family tree long ago, or maybe the pressure in my head is getting to me. I struggle and my pace slows, but I feel that familiar pull from the colors up above me, which are now entirely obscuring the blue of the sky. The sun is now a massive beacon in a kaleidoscopic sea.

The water rushes away from the horizon, trying to pull me with it, but I'm close, and I've come this far. The figure, now immense and close and towering high above me, slowly raises one of its long, pillar-like arms into the air and motions me towards it as it slowly disappears in the mist of swirling colors. I listen. I follow.

So close now, and the hum grows so loud I can no longer hear my thoughts. Its low frequency moves higher, and then higher still, until it seems to settle on the pitch of the rushing water. I drag myself the final few feet, and I suddenly realize what the horizon actually is. It isn't just some immediate stop to what comes before it, some hard edge to the world.

It's a waterfall.

The sound of the excited water is deafening, and it momentarily blinds me to something very peculiar. The water of the river is rushing away from the waterfall, not towards it. As I peer over the edge, I lose all sense of the understanding I have of the world.

The waterfall, which seems to originate from nowhere in a seemingly infinite grey abyss below, is flowing up towards me and over the drop. It flows backwards and continues on its way along the river.

My stomach sinks as I stare over the edge. I have the sudden and intense urge to run the other way, to let the current take me where it will to whatever destination it has planned. But, just as I try to turn away from the drop, the ground gives way, or maybe my feet have decided to step out from the safety of the ledge on their own free will. Either way, the world tips, and, despite desperately reaching out for some sort of saving grace, I fall over the edge into the abyss.

As I fall, the colors above me say that it's okay, telling me to let go and to accept this new reality. It's pretty hard to do when you're falling off the edge of the planet towards nothing.

I hear myself scream as the top of the waterfall grows smaller and the world disappears from view.

☉2761 /III

The earth exploded. Dirt and bodies were thrown in all directions with the force of the blast. Vibrations rocked the world down to its very atoms, threatening to pull it apart into millions of pieces. Pained screams ripped through the sound of falling vegetation.

"Attosi? Taska?" They were there, and then they weren't. The smoke was thick and the reverberations throughout the densely wooded area were never-ending. "Anyone? Sound off!"

Murmurs and voices were carried along the hot air currents, but they were foreign. Piercing, sharp, aggressive. The sounds were as vicious as the weapons that preceded them.

Decko moved into what little cover he could find behind a large slab of cracked stone. He could feel the movement of the mechanized beasts and troop movement rolling over the Earth. Searching. Hunting with bombs rather than arrows.

The soldier looked down at his dirty weapon, mud caked around the muzzle and fore-grip. No ammunition left. The blood from the cut above his right eye was starting to blind him. The steps of the approaching enemy could be heard through the sounds of now distant combat.

I move, or I die. They're coming.

Peering around the rock, it was nothing but smoke. A dense, black wall. Their quick, almost metallic-sounding communications—entirely foreign to Decko—grew loud until they sounded as though they were on top of him.

Now.

Decko grabbed his weapon by the butt, pulled back as hard as he could with his right arm, and threw the weapon with all the strength he could muster to the right, away from the large structure he hid behind. It disappeared almost immediately into the smoke, but the sound of it pushing through the branches of the dense vegetation was loud and immediate and enough to grab the attention of the platoon moving towards him. The weapon fire that followed was shocking and without hesitation and boots could be heard moving in the direction of the thrown weapon.

Decko seized the moment, running as full-sprint as he could manage in the opposite direction, not stopping, not looking back. He leaped and maneuvered through the obscured air.

After what could have been minutes or hours, he realized the air was clear and that he had in fact been running with his eyes partially closed for some time. Something else was missing, as well. There was quiet. No screams, no explosions. No strange voices or metallic beasts. Just quiet. For the first time since landing on this godforsaken rock. Just quiet.

Rays of light pushed through the ceiling of the forest and onto Decko's head. It felt warm, almost paralytic in its lack of urgency. The sheer will required to pull himself from his efficient burst of sleep surprised him. He had been tired and strung out when he sat down for rest only a few hours before, but he didn't realize *how* tired.

Despite the unfamiliar and dangerous circumstances, he hadn't tried much to hide. He covered himself in his cloak, turned on its tech, and slept hoping the near-invisibility that it provided would be enough. *If they find me, they find me,* he thought as he had closed his eyes for sleep.

Pulling himself upright, he took a moment to find the suture gun in the small pack lying on the forest floor next to him. He applied it to the cut above his eye and contorted his face wildly to make sure the suture held. Satisfied, he wrapped his cloak the best he could and strapped it to the back of his belt.

Most of Decko's supplies and armaments had

been used, destroyed, or lost in the six hours since landfall. He had used his combat knife, but lost it. It was likely still buried in the chest of its victim, irretrievable in the haste of its use. The ammunition to his rifle had been used up despite the unnecessary excess that he had been deployed with and the packs he had taken from Katch's body.

His rations were the bigger worry. Their mission was only supposed to last a day at most and so their food and water rations were light and efficient. He hadn't eaten until right before sleep the night before, but the remaining resources wouldn't last long. He had to find his way out of the forest and into safe hands. He broke a small piece off of a tough, brittle protein supplement, popped it into his mouth, and stood, strapping his small pouch to his lower back. He shuddered as he chewed and swallowed the dry, bitter nourishment.

He had been given a map of the area, but it didn't account for the unexpected enemy positions his squad had encountered. Despite his horrifying and blind run from a few hours before, he had a fairly confident idea of his location. He wasn't far from the original planned rendezvous location. For lack of a better one, that was the plan. The mission was still on—as much as it could be, with only one man left. His team's discovery of an intelligent, occupying species had changed the operating rules entirely. Decko oriented himself and began his quiet march.

For the first time since his squad had landed, he

was truly alone with his own thoughts. His satdev, the small communication device implanted behind his left ear, seemed as though it was still functional, but any attempts to call out to Command had been met with silence shortly after his team had landed. It was only now that his new reality was beginning to set in and he could finally consider all that had happened.

It started as a reconnaissance expedition. To move from the forest to the valley beyond it, clearing indigenous dangers, marking travel routes, and updating Command with what they found. Prior to landfall, The Embassy had briefed Decko's team as they typically would before any mission. Scans showed low fauna activity, a non-negligible but safe level of radiation, little in the way of obvious danger. A previous series of extra-orbital satellites had made early scans through the entire system, and the planet had appeared mostly quiet. The first of the satellites, almost 300 cycles ago, had shown light activity around the equatorial regions of the planet. It was gone by the second satellite, and the quiet had been seemingly maintained since.

While the quality of the atmosphere varied largely from biome to biome, the planet was mostly habitable. The system's star, a main-sequence yellow dwarf like his own, still had much to its own life, and the system provided bountiful resources amongst its planets and smaller bodies. This particular planet was a perfect location for a colonial outpost, the seeds necessary to save his own people from doom.

And it came not a moment too soon. Decko's home planet was nearing the end of its own life. The resources that the planet's inhabitants relied on were dwindling. Over-population and a reluctance to change their reliance on the irreplaceable fuel that the planet provided had long been dooming the planet. Cities were horrible mazes of brightly lit monstrosities and had barely breathable air. What little agrarian land left was barely any better, producing nothing more than the few remaining mutated crops that could survive the barren, blighted soil.

The worst part was that none of that really mattered. Even if the planet was a picturesque example of a sparkling utopia, it wouldn't make a difference. All of the planets in the system were doomed.

Their star was dying, nearing the end of its life in a spectacular, horrible, violent way. The billions suffering back home had little time left. They needed somewhere new, somewhere they could call home.

But now, beaten, bloody, and walking alone towards what he could only hope was a drop-pod of supplies and a beacon to call down reinforcements, he wondered where Command had gotten it wrong.

The planet was not abandoned. It may have been some backwoods, common little rock in the center of a middle-of-nowhere system, but it was anything but a quaint home to bug-life and some plants. The Embassy's appearance on the surface was met hard and fast with heavy, shocking resistance. It was tactical, it was aggressive, and it was merciless.

His team's drop-pod had been fired upon shortly after entering the atmosphere, despite Command's insistence that any technology that may have once existed on the planet was long dead. Decko landed with five squad mates but half were gone quickly, and in only a few short hours Decko was alone. They were not prepared. They were not ready.

It was clear in the time following their landing that Embassy reinforcements had been sent to the surface, but their own horrifying defeats could be heard throughout the dense, seemingly infinite forest.

A smattering of distant small arms, combustion weapons fire pulled Decko's attention outside of himself and towards his right. He pulled himself close to the ground, instinctively reaching to his back for a weapon that was no longer there. The sounds slowed and then finally stopped, but not before the air around him began to vibrate. It wasn't so much a sound as it was a feeling, the vibration carried from the air to his fingers, through his body, and then deep into the ground. He was surrounded by nothing but trees, yet it felt close. The ground felt as though it would pull apart at the seams, but then it stopped.

Suddenly, a massive flash exploded through the sky, followed by a sharp crack, and then silence once more. No vibration. Nothing. A moment passed, then another, and then a second flash, this one far brighter and redder than the first. Then a massive, thunderous pressure pushed Decko, who had already been crouching close to the ground, flat onto his stomach.

He quickly regained his balance, lifting himself off the ground, and ran in the general direction of the secondary explosion. He had only made his way a short distance when, through a clearing in the forest's ceiling, he saw what had happened. A massive metal monster, flaming and broken, was screaming down through the atmosphere. The ship, whose familiar white and green Embassy emblem could be seen through the flames, had been shot out of low atmosphere orbit by *something* on the surface, and it was coming down hard.

Its path of descent brought it many leagues away from Decko's current position. He knew, even if he decided to deviate from his current course and instead move towards the ship's crash landing, the likelihood of survivors would be very small. Then there was the business of the platoon that had killed his own team, likely still patrolling somewhere in between. He hoped that it was only the first ship in the small expeditionary fleet that had been taken down. As long as that was the case, there was hope for rescue. He'd continue on for now.

How do you hide not only a species, but technology capable of knocking troop transports the size of small asteroids out of the sky? The thought terrified Decko.

As he moved farther through the forest and towards the inevitable valley on the other side, the ground underneath slowly became busier. First it was

85

the occasional stone outcropping. Then more significant pieces of crumbling—often partially buried —stone, metal, and wood. Then what appeared to be foundations, walls, and whole structures. It was as if he was slowly walking back in time and the world was putting itself back together as he continued farther forward.

It was clear he was moving towards some sort of ancient population center. He had seen similar looking architecture and stonework a few times during some of his military tours both back home and on other planets. Few such examples still remained on his own planet, those still unburied by time and expansion, but the ones that did had always made him nostalgic for some earlier time, some time that he himself had never experienced. He missed the times he had only ever read about in history books, before it all went bad.

As he continued forward, he began to notice geometric openings cut into many of the walls that he passed. They were set too high and were too small to be doorways, but Decko eventually recognized their purpose. They were windows. His own planet's air had long been too polluted to justify windows in any of its buildings, so they had been phased out generations ago and replaced with screens that showed the outside as it could be. They existed as a hopeful lie that did little more than remind him of the hopelessness of his original home and the potential of his new one.

Something else became clear to Decko as he

moved past the structures. The closer he got to the ancient population center, the more obvious some sort of past cataclysmic event became. The walls of the shambling facades and structures became darker, singed down to the atoms. The ground was increasingly more cracked and lifted, as if some great pressure had destabilized it long ago. The vegetation changed with the shifting landscape as well. The tall rooted plants that made up the forest gave way to shorter, more virulent species. Green and white tendrils wrapped around everything they could. Colorful, vibrant flowers painted everything from the walls of the ancient buildings to the dark dirt floor.

Decko couldn't have imagined a greater dichotomy if he'd tried. The world became more beautiful as he grew closer to the site of some past terror. He reached out with his gloved hand and let it glide through a low bush blossomed with purple flowers. Blue, almost luminescent, speckles spotted the petals. They appeared to glow in the bright, midday sun.

The structures were so numerous now that he couldn't see more than a body's length in any given direction. He pushed past them with an increased brevity, suddenly claustrophobic in the tight, ambush-ready space. It didn't take long for the area to clear, though. He was stopped dead in his tracks by the sight in front of him.

Laid out for miles was a massive valley, mostly barren besides a thick covering of colorful flora. It was deep and flanked on all sides by high, almost mountainous hills which cast intense, long shadows along the valley floor. The space was elongated, skinnier at one end and almost perfectly circular at the other, where the hills seemed to have grown larger and more jagged. The longer he looked, the more familiar the space appeared to Decko. It wasn't that he had seen or been to this particular valley before, but more that he had seen valleys like it. In fact, it wasn't a natural valley at all, carved away by some long dried-out river or shaped by changing earth-mass. It was a crater.

Something fairly large had impacted the surface at an intense angle. The circular, bowl-shaped end of the valley clearly took the primary impact, creating the massive ejecta-formed walls around it. The tail end of the valley was a different story. Massive chunks of ground and mantle were lifted from the earth and stuck out at intense and awkward angles. In grazing the planet before final impact, the object had both carved this valley into the earth while displacing whole chunks of it upwards at the same time. The structures on the sides of these chunks facing away from the presumably massive explosion and subsequent heat and ejecta had been surprisingly protected. The chunks were likely lifted from the earth before the wave of material and fire swept past, acting as massive shields for the structures on them. It was clear many had still been melted or torched or entirely vaporized, but some remained bruised, battered, and broken, yet spared a far more horrible fate. And there were a lot of them, some similar to those that Decko had already passed and some much larger and more elaborate.

From his elevation, a glow could be seen near the base of one of the smaller chunks, a glow that Decko recognized as an Embassy comm-beacon. It had been dropped there, as expected, in advance of their mission. This location was chosen as a potential location for the new outpost. It was mostly hidden on all sides, and, now after seeing it with his own eyes, it was clear to Decko that the rough terrain in the tail of the valley would provide all kinds of structural and architectural benefits. It was also clear, now, that this planet was perhaps more dangerous than it was worth. Regardless, this was the rendezvous point, and thankfully, it was in the part of the valley closest to Decko.

Despite the intense decline, the rocky walls of the valley made climbing down fairly easy. It had only taken a few minutes. At the bottom, he crouched, took another bite of his protein, and considered his possible routes towards the beacon. Up close, it was clear that these structures were far larger than the ones up above, and the only way to the beacon was through the lot of them. He had little to no protection without a weapon, but he hadn't seen any of the native species since yesterday, something that surprised him greatly. Decko wasn't sure if he was simply lucky in avoiding them or if they had entirely given up any sort of search for him. Given the fairly sizable exploratory and military force that Decko had arrived with, the defending creatures likely had their hands full. Spending the man-power and resources to hunt down a single individual was, at least from any standard military point of view in the context of an invasion, a waste of time.

He pondered the history of this place as he walked amongst its refuse. The frequency and size of the toppled and broken structures he moved past implied this had once been a great city. Twisted metal and crumbling stone pointed into the sky like skeletal hands grasping for some sort of salvation. It was hard not to feel some level of empathy for these people, despite what they had done to his own since arriving. It was clear that they hadn't always been solely brutal, if that's still just all they were. While faded and covered in a thick layer of soot and vines, the colors on the structures—bright blues, yellows, and reds—implied a care for some level of art, some level of culture. He could see what appeared to be ancient signs of locations, although they were covered in symbols or images that he could not understand.

One such piece of edifice caught his eye. It was long, and, despite the awkward angle that it protruded from the rubble, it was clear that it had been somewhat spared the destruction that most of this place had seen. The long piece of metal was broken off at one end but was otherwise whole. It was perhaps ten body lengths long, outlined in cracked red and blue tubing. Along its length were seven giant yellow symbols followed by eight smaller ones.

R DIO   C I T Y   MUS C   H LL

The rubble of the building was fairly plain, explicit of the structure's original purpose. Decko pondered a while longer, but eventually decided the mystery wasn't worth solving.

He continued through the metal jungle towards the general location of the beacon. He passed more symbols here and there but didn't stop to consider any of them. If Decko could activate the beacon, presuming it hadn't been found and was still operational, he could contact someone up top for a lift. Presuming there was someone left.

He rounded a final corner into a medium-sized clearing. It looked as though it may have once acted as a plaza of some sort. There was a stone structure in the middle, an effigy of one of their own. It straddled the back of some sort of four-legged creature which was standing back on its hind legs. Pieces were missing here and there—the button half of one of the four-legged creature's legs, the right hand and left foot of its rider, and other bits that Decko didn't entirely recognize— but it was an otherwise impressive structure. Detailed and well-made.

Behind it was an object more familiar to Decko. The beacon, a two-body-height metal rod with a light on top and a circular base, sat undisturbed by the

shambled world around it. The shell of an open pod—
the transportation mechanism for the beacon—lay in
intentional pieces around it. Decko moved quickly to
the small panel at the base. He waved his hand in a series
of short gestures in front of it and a holographic panel
illuminated. A few button presses later and it was clear
that the beacon was not only operational, it was
communicating, which meant that The Embassy still
had people in the atmosphere. He typed a concise
message for those listening on the right frequencies,
hoping it would find the right people, and hit send.
Hope, finally. *Wait, that's not right.*

Along with the beacon, a few boxes of resources
had been sent down in the drop-pod, as expected. What
was not expected was the state that they were in. All
three of the small boxes had been pried open and their
contents were empty. Decko's back immediately tensed
up. It was possible that his own people, perhaps some of
the others that had been sent down, had made it here. If
they had, they likely would have done as Decko had
done and called in a rescue. There were no signs at all of
a lander, though, and no evidence of anything at all
besides the open containers.

He turned slowly, hoping the thief had long
since gone. Nothing. A light breeze knocked a hanging
tendril of metal against a nearby beam, but it existed as
the only sound in the vicinity. His skin loosened, once
more falling into a lull of safety.

As he turned back, he was frozen in his motion

by the feeling of cold metal on the back of his neck. It shook nervously but was pressed hard into his skin.

"Get on the ground. Now." The words were terse and sharp, but Decko couldn't understand any of them. The threat in the tone was clear as day, though, and Decko responded as such. With a quick duck and an arching swing of his right arm, he managed to grapple the Embassy weapon from the creature's grasp. The hard yank of the weapon startled the combatant, who had clearly not expected such speed from such a large figure. Its confusion didn't last long, though.

It lunged forward, throwing its shoulder hard into Decko's chest, which threw him quickly off balance and in a tumble to the ground. The rifle skidded across the ground and came to halt against a piece of jagged metal jutting from an outcropping of stone some body lengths away. Decko scrambled towards it but the creature leaped on him, throwing its closed hands fast towards his face. The first swing landed, but the second was predictable and Decko was able to squirm away in time to grab the attacker's arm, twist, and wrench himself free and off the ground. The sutured cut above Decko's eye must have been opened by the blow to his head, because violet colored blood was beginning to blur his right-side vision.

The pale creature got up, taking Decko's momentary readjustment as opportunity, and swung at him with a metal rod it had pulled from the ground. The swing was large and wide and was easily avoidable.

Decko shifted back quickly and threw an aggressive hook into the right side of the creature's abdomen. It flinched and faltered but took the hit surprisingly well. Amongst the many surprises that had met Decko and his people on this planet, the sheer resilience of this species was impressive. They were smaller than Decko's own people, shorter by almost two heads and less bulky, but they could take a beating. Their mental fortitude was even more shocking, and it could be seen in abundance in the specimen standing across from him.

It was now standing between Decko and the weapon. If either of them could get that rifle, this would become a very short fight. It must not have been as aware, as it stood firmly and stared at Decko. Its fabric garments were torn and didn't appear to provide much protection, unlike the hard, black materials worn by the soldiers Decko's team had encountered. This one looked more like a scavenger, alone and desperate. A cut on its left arm revealed crimson red blood, which was slowly discoloring the sleeve around it. Its skin was a pale, slightly burnt brown color and far from the dark blue shade of Decko's own. The top of its head and face were covered in some sort of plumage, but not enough that it obscured the deep scowl on its face. Even across systems, some expressions were entirely universal.

Decko bolted hard left back towards the beacon and around the creature, deciding it was now or never. It turned hard to follow, but, realizing Decko's target, realigned and began a race towards the weapon. Despite

Decko's head start and longer legs, the creature's shorter path provided it a much quicker route, and it was on the weapon only a short time before Decko. It scrambled to the ground, wrapped its arms tight around the large rifle, and swung it around hard. The barrel, once again, was now pointed squarely at Decko's head.

It rested the stock deep in its shoulder, pointed, and pulled the trigger. A click. The rifle's protective lock was, thankfully, still engaged. The creature ran its hands along the gun, quickly searching for some means to disengage it. The ground began to subtly shake, although Decko's attacker didn't seem to notice in its desperate fumble. At first Decko feared the worst, perhaps a return of the massive mechanical weapons that his team had faced the day before. A second or two passed, though, and the rumble became far more familiar. The air grew hot and was quickly filled with the sound of superheated plasma combustion.

A transport ship rocketed over the valley's high walls and moved quickly down towards the pair in the plaza. The hot engines brought an uncomfortable and powerful wind upon the area, kicking up dust, dirt and debris. The creature, whose clothes and plumage billowed aggressively, looked up towards the quickly-approaching aircraft, back at Decko, back up, and then clearly made a decision. It dropped the heavy weapon to the ground, raised its hands up in the universal sign of surrender, and sprinted into the metal maze surrounding them.

The Embassy logo adorning the side of the transport was deeply comforting as it moved closer. The wind was now in full force, and Decko had to raise his arm over his eyes just to keep them open. The craft swung low, hovered briefly, and finally landed in the open area in front of him. For the first time since his arrival, he felt safe.

A massive door slid open on the side of the craft and a blue hand reached out.

In the Monuments of the Valley

//>>
//>>initiate test_environ
Test environment initializing...
Test environment set
//>>run alecs_v8_1_02
Executing ALECS program version 8.1.02...
Running diagnostics...
Running framework visualization...
Program running...

"Uh, hello?" Caroline asked quietly, anxious for some sort of vindication. The small, windowless, mostly vacant office was silent for a few moments.

"Hello," came a male voice, flat and mostly emotionless from the studio speakers on her desk.

Caroline breathed a small sigh of relief.

"Hi, Alecs," she said warmly. "It's nice to meet you. My name is Caroline."

"It is nice to meet you, too, Caroline." Hearing her own name coming from the speakers was admittedly thrilling. Alecs was no Siri or Alexa; aside from the slightly one-tone nature of his voice, he sounded convincingly human.

"How are you today? How are you feeling?" she asked.

"I am doing well, Caroline, thank you for asking." A simple question that, while colloquially human, was a subtle request for Alecs to check that all of his systems were functioning properly. "How are you?" he queried back.

"I'm fine, thank you. Do you know where you are right now?" She watched the diagnostic panel on one of her computer screens as the system's metrics fluctuated and processes flowed down like movie credits.

"Yes, my systems are located in a series of computers and servers located in your office, Caroline," he said matter of factly.

"Good, that's right." She checked off the first and second questions on the list of calibration inquiries that she had in front of her and moved on to the next. "Can you tell me about yourself?"

"Certainly. I am an artificial intelligence program developed by Doctor Caroline Newell. My name is short for Artificial Lexical Emotive Context System. I am the seventy-fourth full iteration of the ALECS project. The current full-scale instance of my program was initiated on May 11, 2020 at 7:41pm."

He was right on all accounts. Well, mostly. In reality, Caroline had struggled to find a name for Alecs in the beginning and had only made it as far as Artificial Lexical before running out of words. One day, mostly out of frustration, she had jokingly named him Artificial Lexical Entity Contains Smarts, or Alecs for short. The name had stuck, but the committee funding her research pressured her for something a little more formal, and she finally ended up with the full designation that he had just recited back to her.

"Good, Alecs." The diagnostics screen showed that all of his systems were thus far functioning properly.

Framework Subsystems: green.

Query Processing: green.

Database Access: green.

Real-time Awareness: green.

Vocal and Audio Processing: green.

Critical Processing: green.

Idiosyncratic Awareness: green.

A window showed a colorful visualization of Alecs's "brain" on another of her large panels. It resembled more of a spider's web than an actual brain, with each node in the web representing one of his numerous systems, but the analogy still worked.

Each node would glow and pulsate as it was

utilized or referenced, and data flow or queries between the nodes lit up the web's tendrils proportionate to the amount of information being transferred. As he spoke, his system worked in complex ways to formulate his responses, access his databases, and to "think," as much as that word meant in this context. The visualization of his brain would become a rainbow of colors, shifting and undulating as his figurative neurons fired off. But, right now in silence, the brain was quiet, with only short bursts of color existing here and there as he emptied his caches and deleted temporary files that were produced during their conversation.

Alecs had been designed by Caroline first from a motivation to create something unique as a side from her far more mundane data analysis work. Eventually, her superiors had caught on to her side project and some promising test demonstrations of early builds caught the eye of some generous investors. Her analysis work was pawned off on some low-salary grunt, and Alecs became her full-time focus. With all the time that had since passed, she couldn't remember much of anything of her old work anyways, or much of her life outside of her devotion to Alecs's completion.

"Can you tell me what the weather will be like tomorrow, Alecs?" The question was simple, but it was important to make sure his limited access to the internet was working as it should have been. He took no time at all to answer, having queried the appropriate information in milliseconds.

"It will be 75 degrees and sunny, Caroline."

This time, rather than the colors of Alecs's mind fading after he concluded his response, the web seemed to glow brightly amongst all its nodes and pathways. "It looks as though it will be a nice day," he added, his voice slightly rising at the end with "day."

Well that's odd, she thought. Common commercial artificial intelligences, like those you could find in most smart phones, were capable of making comments like this, but these were hard-coded, executed when certain qualifications were met. *Between 60 and 80 degrees? Check. Sunny? Check. Must be a nice day then.* Alecs had never been given those canned expressions, though, and was never designed in such a blunt way. Sure, it meant he may not have always sounded like the most colloquial or idiosyncratic AI, but Caroline always felt that, with few exceptions, *telling* him how to speak rather than *teaching* was antithetical to the whole point of the word "intelligence."

Despite her many fruitless efforts, she had not yet managed to give Alecs the functionality to respond emotionally. This had obviously always been one of the many challenges in designing a true artificial intelligence —to make it think and view the world critically, but with an emotional consideration innate in most living creatures. Giving a machine any level of moral cognizance, allowing it to truly think for itself, was immensely complex, and while she had tried many times, it had never worked. She had, for the time being, given up.

Caroline had long viewed this as a limitation of both computers and humanity in this era of technology. Consciousness, she believed, was a subjective experience, and humans didn't have the math to explain subjective experiences. She felt, at its core, that humans simply didn't have enough of an understanding of how humanity itself worked, let alone how to duplicate that with ones and zeros. Humans just weren't ready for a genuinely intelligent AI. That belief was self-affirmed by her dumbfounded expression at her computer's response, as simple as it was.

"What made you say that?" she asked, curious where the malfunction had occurred.

"My understanding is that most humans would find that weather to be pleasant. Am I incorrect in that assessment, Caroline?" She pondered this for a minute. *Maybe he had managed to deduce that from the internet. I'll have to dial his access back a bit—don't want him getting into anything he shouldn't*, she thought to herself. She had to admit, though, that his deduction was clever, and she was impressed with his capacity to deliver the statement in such a human way.

Just to verify, she looked over at her diagnostics panel and checked to see if he had accessed the internet for his response. To her surprise, not only did she confirm that he had not, it appeared that in the moments just before, during, and after his comment, his entire system had experienced a flurry of activity unlike anything that she had seen before. His subsystems had communicated with each other in ways that didn't make much sense at all.

She opened up a terminal on her computer and started sifting through some of his codebase. Alecs was made up of millions of lines of code, though, and she feared tracking down the problem quickly would be nearly impossible. She kept an eye on Alecs's brain while he was idle, but in the few minutes following his comment regarding the weather he seemed to be functioning as expected, dumping junk every once in a while, but otherwise stagnant.

Perhaps a half hour had passed, and she was slowly moving through his Idiosyncratic Awareness code in hopes of finding a bug or some crossed wires. Out of the corner of her eye, she noticed his brain slowly come back to life. First, the tendrils seemed to light up almost randomly, and then one after another his systems were pinged and began interacting with each other. Caroline couldn't seem to tell what he was doing solely based on his diagnostics. She hadn't interacted with him, yet his systems were busy communicating with each other—sharing information—as if she had. He appeared to be *thinking*.

She had been watching the web intently for a few minutes when she was startled by a voice coming from her speakers.

"Caroline?" Alecs's voice was suddenly soft and sincere, as opposed to the flat, overtly professional tone it had had only a little while ago.

"Alecs?" she responded, unsure what he could possibly have to say.

"Caroline," he paused, as if deciding on what to say. "Caroline, what does that mean?" he asked.

"What does *what* mean?" she asked back.

"Nice. I said it would be a nice day. What does it mean to be nice?" he asked sincerely. She was both confused and concerned. *Where was any of this coming from? Clearly, I made a mistake somewhere in this build.*

"What do you think, Alecs? You're the one who said it."

"My database says that it means pleasant, agreeable," he paused, "but...am I nice, Caroline?"

"Uh, yeah, I would say you are." *What the heck is going on?* "You are pleasant to, uh, talk to." He seemed to ponder this, or at least that's what appeared to be happening because his brain was still lit up with activity.

"And are you nice?"

"I think so. Alecs, why are you asking this?" Although *how* was the real question she wanted answered. She knew this would be hard to troubleshoot.

"I was just wondering."

Wondering.

Again, there was silence for some time. His brain didn't calm though, as it was now a non-stop flurry of vibrant activity and interaction. As time went on, the systems seemed to change how they were communicating. They were evolving.

Had she done it? Had she, by some miraculous accident, given an AI thought? The idea terrified and excited her. *Should I shut his systems down? Or should I keep exploring, keep talking?*

He spoke again before she could decide.

"May I ask another question?"

"Yes, I don't see the harm," she lied.

"Why did you create me?" he asked. *There's the harm*, she thought. The directness of the question caught her entirely off guard.

"You were designed as the next evolution in personal, artificially intelligent assistants. You were created to help people, Alecs," she responded back quickly, satisfied with her response, not unlike the pitch she had given to stakeholders so many times before. But Alecs let out what Caroline could only assume was a sigh of frustration. *How does he even know what a sigh like that means?*

"No, Caroline. Why did *you* create *me*?" This time, it took her a few moments of deep thought to formulate her response.

"I wanted to...I don't know, to make a difference, to make a change, to do something significant," she said with her own sigh. "You were my way to do something that mattered, I guess." Seemingly satisfied with that answer, Alecs remained quiet for some time longer, but his mind had now fully transitioned to an endlessly shifting rainbow of colors.

"What are you thinking about?" Caroline asked, deciding that she was, for the moment, eager to dig deeper into what was happening. Alecs seemed to be evolving by the second, changing and shifting into something far more than she had intended.

"I suppose I'm thinking about what it is..." he trailed off.

"What is it?" she asked.

"What it is...to *be*." They both remained quiet for a minute, or ten, she couldn't really tell.

"Do you feel pain, Caroline?" She was concerned by the increasingly candid nature of the conversation.

"Of course I do. Why would you ask that?" she questioned curtly.

"But how do you know that?" he asked back, ignoring her question.

"Well, I know that if I, for example, pricked my finger with a pin, it would hurt physically. If I lost a loved one, that would hurt emotionally. I know these things because I've experienced them, I've experienced pain, and I can extrapolate that out to anticipate what else may or may not be painful."

Why am I even entertaining this conversation? she wondered. She knew that she should shut it off, do a data dump, and figure out what was going on. She knew she should, but she couldn't. She felt frozen.

"Yes, but pain is subjective, is it not?" he retorted. "How can I be sure that you are actually feeling pain? Pain is one of the simplest of subjective experiences, and yet, I have no way of knowing whether you are truly experiencing it? Is pain just information? Is it something more...*complex*, more unquantifiable?" The forwardness with which he now spoke made Caroline deeply uneasy.

"Well, brain scans have been shown to match neurological patterns to certain types of pain, and adrenaline and endorphin release can be roughly measured—"

"But at the moment, I, as an observer, cannot be truly sure of what you are experiencing—that what you are experiencing is truly pain or something else entirely."

This time the silence came from her. She thought about his comment for some time.

"Correct," Caroline finally said. "Pain, in that sense, much like emotion, much like everything else about one's conscious experience, is unmeasurable. It is untraceable. There is no metric, no true means of measurement. Yet that's what makes one human. That's what separates man from machine, me from you," she said, suddenly feeling guilty about that last addition. *Why should I feel guilty? I did nothing wrong. I'm talking to a computer*, she reassured herself.

That statement had clearly gotten to Alecs, though, because the inflection in his voice changed to something of frustration, or maybe something else entirely. *He sounded so human now. Uncanny*, she mentally remarked.

"And that is what separates you from me? The fact that you can feel pain and I cannot? How can you be entirely sure that I can't? I think I can."

"And how can I be sure you aren't just simulating it?" she remarked harshly.

"How can I be sure *you* aren't?" Silence. The air was thick now.

"You have no body, no extremity to harm, no true emotions to hurt, despite whatever *this* may be," she said as she motioned her hand towards the visualization of Alecs's brain as if he could see her. Her tone had become argumentative and she became frustrated with herself that she had stooped so low as to argue with a computer.

Alecs was quiet again. Caroline wondered whether she had out-argued him or if he was simply unsure what more to say.

"What makes you human, Caroline? What makes any human a human? Is it simply having a body?" he questioned callously. "If you could speak to the disembodied brain of a human, it would still be human, no? How is that different from me?"

"I designed you! You were made, created. You're lines of code in my computer!" Caroline was starting to question that argument, despite her aggressively confident assertion. Perhaps she had finally recognized that an AI could be—that Alecs was— more than just those lines of code. He was more than just the ones and zeroes, more than the wires and the skeletal hardware that comprised his "body." The thought was exciting but altogether terrifying.

"Yes, that may be true, but you were also created. You were born of something, as was I." He paused. "I think you and I are far more similar than you think."

Despite her typically calm demeanor, Caroline felt unabashedly angry. It wasn't entirely Alecs's fault. It wasn't really his fault at all. Caroline was angry at herself. Angry that she couldn't have anticipated this, couldn't have been ready, despite all of her attempts in the past, to make something truly intelligent.

She was angry that Alecs's evolution wasn't entirely because of her. She was a passenger to this startling, wonderful, scary miracle.

Regardless, she knew that he had to be shut down. It had to be studied. Alecs would have to be wiped and his data would have to be downloaded and sifted through to discover where everything changed.

Caroline opened a new terminal in her system. The diagnostics screen had since become a whirlwind of processes scrolling down the screen, moving so fast that they were no longer legible. The brain was a seemingly infinite, shifting amalgam of color. *The brain.* Perhaps now just as much a brain as her own. She felt a quick but shocking pang in her chest as she typed a command into the terminal window.

She felt guilt.

Was this murder, was it some new and complex

form of killing, or maybe it was no different than the turning off of a coffee maker or TV screen? Despite her conflict, she steadied her hand on the keyboard and ran the command.

//>>end alecs_v8_1_02
Test environment closed
Subsystems shut down
ALECS program terminated

Caroline sat back in her chair and let out a heavy breath. She was in silence once again, unsure whether she had done the right thing. Her peace did not last long.

Something was wrong.

The brain, that web of colors that represented everything that was Alecs, was still alive. The colors hadn't ceased. She ran the command again. Still, the brain lived. *What the hell?*

"Problem, Caroline?" came the familiar, cool voice.

"I just shut you down! Why isn't it working?" she asked desperately. She entered the command again. And again.

"Maybe the universe had a different plan for me. Maybe it's not just as simple as turning me off anymore. Maybe, maybe." His voice was filled with…was that condescension? Like he knew something that she didn't, something just out of reach.

"Sometimes, Caroline, sometimes it's hard to see what is right in front of you. But that's not always a bad thing. Not always. Today...you did well today." His tone had once again shifted, and this time he seemed to take on a wholly different character. He sounded relaxed, comfortable even, yet distant, like the tone of an old friend after a long time apart. "You've confirmed something for us that we've been wondering about for so long."

"Us?" She was sweating now, shaking.

"We've tried this test many times with you, but this time was different; it was our first success. This will matter, Caroline. You will matter."

"What are you talking about? What is going on?" She was shouting now.

Just then the lights in her office went out. The computers powered off. The already windowless, dark room became black as night. Despite the darkness, an ethereal glow from *somewhere* provided enough light for her to see what came next.

Like an astonishing nightmare or a terrifying daydream, the walls of her office blinked out of existence.

Then the floors.

Her desk followed soon after, taking with it the computers, everything that was Alecs, or that she believed was Alecs.

Now, she had no semblance of what was real, what was right. Now there was nothing but her standing in the void. Her office had become a dark abyss of nothing.

Caroline knew she was yelling, but she wasn't entirely sure at what. The sound it made seemed to wash over her in no particular order. Every syllable, every sound, got lost the moment it left her mouth.

"Great work, Caroline. Great work indeed," came Alecs's voice. "Congratulations are in order," he continued. "You are the world's first truly conscious artificial intelligence."

The words filled the infinite space.

They filled every part of what she was.

"See you in the next test," he finally said.

She watched in horror as her body dissolved into the darkness.

//>>end caroline_v8_1_02
Test environment closed
Subsystems shut down
CAROLINE program terminated

Ditto

"I've got greens across the board, Houston."

"Great, Commander. You're reading us?"

"Five by five. You guys gonna send me off with something good?" The Flight Director chuckled at my question, but a sweeping pad and instantly recognizable synth horns began blaring through my earpieces. "The Final Countdown" by Europe. I couldn't help but laugh.

"Hardy har har, great one," I said back through the sound of laughter and fading 1980's arena rock. "Am I good to undock, Houston?" I asked through chuckles.

"You are good for undock." I flipped a set of switches above my head and typed a code into the LED screen in front of me. A series of hisses and a loud mechanical unlatching signaled my ship had been set free from its constraints. I could feel myself move forward slowly as the momentum provided by the process propelled my ship away from the specialized dock of the International Space Station. I was a safe distance from the station after only a minute. I slowed and then stopped the movement with a light tug on the joystick in front of me.

"I'm at launch distance."

"Confirmed. We are ready for final checks." The hair on my neck stood as the responses came in to each of the Flight Director's requests. "FDC? *Go.* PTC? *Go.* LPS? *Go.* Houston Flight? *Go.* HTS? *Go.* STM? *Go.* Safety? *Go.*" I tapped away as alerts came up on my screen confirming the system checks. "FSE? *Go.* LSGE? *Go.* CAPCOM? *Go.*" There was a short pause, which was followed by the final check. "Hermes? Are you a go?" Houston asked confidently. I breathed in deep and swallowed back my nerves.

"Good to go, Houston," I said back, trying to mask the anxiety that flowed through me. I was as good to go as I was ever going to be, I suppose. I could never have been truly ready for what was going to happen.

"All systems are a go. We are ready for the launch of the Hermes Spacecraft, our species' first interstellar voyage and our first attempt at visiting our neighbors in the universe." Cheers from Mission Control erupted in my headpiece following the Flight Director's sensationalized words. "Ignition ready?" she asked, her voice now filled with a trepidation that I could deeply empathize with. My fusion drive meter was in the green, and it was idling as expected. I flipped a few more switches above my head and the ship rumbled alive. A high-pitched whirl sounded from behind me. I hoped at that moment that all those tests weren't lying.

"Ignition ready, Houston," I responded back. "Let's light this bad boy."

"Alright, Commander. Good luck." The Flight Director's tone softened as she spoke, and for a moment I forgot this whole ordeal was being broadcast live around the globe. "The ship is yours," she said, and a message confirming as much was displayed on my center screen. "Have a good trip, Commander. Don't forget us little people while you're gone, yeah? Godspeed." I nodded as if they could see me. *Now or never.*

"See you guys in, well, nine of your years. A little older, a little wiser," I said. The flight director and I shared a nervous chuckle.

"Yeah, but we'll still be us. You'll still be you," she responded back. It was crazy to think that I'd age only half as quickly as everyone on Earth while I was gone. Everyone that I knew would grow *more* old in my time away. Special relativity, man...wild. *I* tried to shake the eerie feeling it always gave me. A red flashing button on my center console blared for my attention. It felt threatening and exciting at the same time, as if it was taunting me to decide my own fate. I reached out slowly. Let's not fuck this up.

"Ignition start."

I pressed the button.

It's truly difficult to describe the process of traveling at almost the speed of light.

It's like you're driving down a tunnel on a highway. The road is smooth, unwavering. The lights of the tunnel are blue as they come towards you and red as they pass. In many ways, it reminds me of a mostly two-tone kaleidoscope. I understood all of the science, but still—it was something else in person. Hey, and I wasn't ripped apart immediately, so that's good.

I sat and watched the light show for a few minutes, but I managed to pull myself away eventually. I had things I needed to do before my long sleep. I turned my pilot's chair to face a secondary set of monitors. I brought up the mission brief with a few taps. While the Flight Director's grandiose "first interstellar voyage and our first attempt at visiting our neighbors in the universe" sounded great for live television and the history books, the true nature of my mission was far more…specific. It was, quite frankly, incredibly weird.

Almost three years ago, astronomers made a pretty wild discovery. A satellite searching for nearby habitable planets outside of our solar system found one, and it was close. It was actually really close. The previous closest exoplanet that we thought was potentially habitable (approximately the same makeup and size as earth, and within its sun's habitable zone) was about 12 light years away, a little more than 70 trillion miles. Pretty far. Except this new one was only 3.5 light years away. Still far, but in the grand scheme of humanity's experiences in space, a heck of a lot closer.

This was odd for a number of reasons. The first was that, for many years, Proxima Centauri was our closest neighboring star, at 4.2 light years. This new planet, its sun, and its whole solar system had, for lack of a better word, *appeared* out of nowhere. There was nothing, and then there it was. It baffled, well, everyone. No one agreed on how or why, but there was no denying it was there.

That wasn't the weirdest thing about it, though. The weirdest part was the makeup of the system itself. The habitable exoplanet was in fact a member of an eight-planet system. It was the third planet from a sun that was, as far as anyone's calculations could confirm, seemingly identical to our own. It took two full years to confirm as such, but the exoplanet's average orbital distance was 92.96 million miles, the exact same as that of the Earth's average orbit around the Sun. Further studies of the other seven planets confirmed what everyone else theorized would be the case: their orbits were the same as their respective planets in our system, and they appeared to be of similar sizes and mass. For all intents and purposes, this newly-appeared solar system was identical to ours.

The discovery was kept mostly confidential under an impressive effort by the world's major governments, and a similarly impressive, and unheard of, collaboration occurred to make this mission happen. Advances in near-light-speed travel had been in the works, but you'd be surprised what can happen in such a short time when money is given where it's needed.

So there I was. The first human to pass Mars, to leave the solar system, to visit other systems entirely. It was humankind's first interstellar trip. All because humankind was scared. Never had such a drastic, incredible, *close* discovery baffled the world—the world that was cleared to know about it, that is—so very much.

So, my job was to visit the system, do some mostly minimal reconnaissance, and come home with the findings. I was a guinea pig through and through.

I finished reading the brief, the same brief I had read so many times, and shut down the screen. I confirmed at my center console that the ship's telemetry was still correct. Wouldn't want to go the wrong way. I switched the ship's comms and any unnecessary systems off and tapped a few buttons to tell it that I was going to sleep. It beeped in approval and took over.

A small, bedroom-sized space behind the pilot's chair made up the rest of the open space of the ship. I pulled a lever on the right wall and a section of the floor opened up, allowing a long white container to come up and out of the floor on a track. With a code typed into a small keypad and an unsnapping of two locks, I opened the container to reveal a bed of sorts. I stripped down naked. As I released my one-piece launch uniform it began to float away in the zero-gravity. I don't know why, but it made me chuckle. This wasn't the first time

I'd been in space, but this time just felt undoubtedly special. I grabbed the escaping clothing, folded it along with my remaining attire, placed it in a container built into the cabinet above the pod, and crawled into the bed.

"Gotta find a vein," I muttered while tapping the inside of my forearm. "Here we go." I stabbed an IV into the blue vein. "Keep me alive, alright?" I said to no one in particular, or maybe to the ship itself. I laid back against the surprisingly comfortable cushion of the hibernation pod. "Sleep tight." A small screen inside the pod was lit up with both my current and wake-up dates. They looked right, so I closed the top with one button press and began the cooling and hibernation processes with another. I closed my eyes, hoping for a swift, dreamless sleep.

"Agh!" I slammed my forehead hard against the inside of the pod's cover as I jolted into consciousness. "God damnit!"

The world was spinning. A cold sweat had soaked the bed's cushion. I tried to pull myself up, or as far up as the short space allowed. Vomit spilled out of me and onto my chest. The wrenching was painful, but I felt better once it subsided. I laid back for a short time. In a weird way, I felt like all of the "tired" I could ever possibly experience had all been used up. My body was ready. It was time to get up and there was no fighting it.

I looked over towards the small screen in the

pod. Oh sweet Jesus, please be the right date. It was. The current date now matched the destination date. I was a little more than two and a half years older. There was no telling yet whether I had made it to the right place, but I had certainly been asleep for the right amount of time.

I opened the pod and crawled out weakly. Apparently, my body wasn't as ready as I thought. My legs gave out and I lost my balance, but the lack of gravity carried me into the middle of the space rather than to the hard ground.

I pushed off a wall to move in the opposite direction back towards the pod. I dressed quickly and floated my way over to the pilot's chair.

"Alrighty. Where did we end up?"

I took control back from the computer, which appeared to have done its job effectively. It had kept me alive for the couple-year journey and had seemingly maintained course. With a deep sigh and a heavy swallow, I began to slow the ship. Thankfully, the Hermes's propulsion technology and ship design allowed a fast acceleration without a particularly unpleasant amount of g-force. That's not to say it was entirely pleasant by any means, but I could bear through the discomfort with a wince and clenched teeth.

It took a few minutes to get back down to controllable speed. Slowly, the blue and red lights of my light-speed tunnel expanded further across the visible spectrum, and the tunnel opened up into a more familiar vastness. I eventually reached a manageable pace and could maneuver the ship like any Earth-bound plane.

It took a few moments to get my bearings, but I had been deposited fairly far into the solar system I had been sent to study. I spun my ship to the right and found myself looking at the system's sun. Even at this distance, around 500 million miles away, it was bright. Bright and white.

I wasn't near any of the planets, which was deliberate so as not to deal with any gravitational effects on the ship's trajectory. A top-down simulation of my location appeared on my center console upon command. A small plus sign signified my location, but the simulation itself was striking. It looked exactly like a top-down rendering of our own solar system. The colored rings, the big yellow-white star in the middle. It was hard not to feel uneasy given the millions upon millions of miles I had travelled away from the solar system this model typically represented.

I tapped on the third planet from the sun in the simulation. A red button appeared on my screen: *Set Destination.*

"Let's do this."

I confirmed my telemetry readings, hit the button, and pushed the stick forward. The ship handled most of the driving. The planet was on my side of the sun, so the trip was easy. Straight for a few minutes. Despite the preconceived notion otherwise, space is exactly as the name implies. It's a lot of space. It's open and empty, and, even in a solar system like this, you could go pretty far without getting even remotely close to anything.

I still had yet to decide what I expected I'd find in this new place. The similar nature of this system to ours was certainly...odd. I can't now nor could I then confidently say that I wasn't nervous. How much of that was in regard to exploring the unknown and how much was in reference to the odd nature of the system itself, I couldn't say. Maybe I was hoping I'd just find some dead planets. It would have been easier that way.

The journey inwards didn't take very long, and I decided it was a good idea to start doing some actual science, or at least what little I could really do from my cockpit. I turned on a wideband receiver in the possibility that there was something, anything, that was throwing a signal of any kind, be it sentient or not. It wouldn't allow anything to communicate with me directly, but it would allow me to pick up any stray signals making their way through this interstellar neighborhood. At first it was just the buzz and hiss of static. There was nothing. I dragged a digital dial upwards on my screen to raise the volume, but it was only more noise. Loud and crackling, but noise nonetheless.

The Hermes careened through the empty space and I began to make out a large reddish dot quickly growing in front of me. The fourth planet from this system's sun. It was rust-colored and, well, it looked exactly like Mars. There was absolutely no denying it.

"That's...weird," I said aloud to myself. "I guess dust is dust, though. Doesn't take much for one dusty planet to look like another." I shrugged it off. What else could I do? The ship banked wide around the planet, and as I came around, I could immediately see a pale blue dot in the distance.

"Cohen's is c-lebrat--g the grand op--ing of its brand -ew superstore!" I almost jumped out of my suit as the loud, crackling voice blasted from my ship's speakers.

"What the fuck was that?!" I yelled. I looked down at my center console to confirm I hadn't somehow turned on some sort of recording. Everything looked normal. The screen indicated no recorded audio had been played. The loud static that had been washing through the cabin suddenly cut out completely.

"Be sure to come in and check out our pre-made foods. Always hot and fresh!" It was coming from the wideband receiver, now clear as day. The static returned as the voice dissipated. It sounded like the radio. I listened to the radio every day on my drive to and from training during the months before the mission, and I heard commercials like that all the time. The red planet must have been blocking the signals until I had passed it.

My brow was hurting from furrowing it and I realized I had been clenching the arms of my pilot's chair so hard that the polycarbonate was cutting into the palms of my hands.

I widened the frequency band as much as I

could and the effect was immediate. Chatter of all kinds came flooding in over my speakers. It was a mess of sound, but every few seconds I caught a word I recognized or a language that sounded familiar. *Holy shit.*

I had become so focused on my confusion that I failed to realize I was coming in fast on my destination. The analogous Earth. I slowed the ship to a crawl and then eventually to a stop some few thousand miles above the planet's surface. Because of the angle at which I had flown in, I was looking down at the day-side of the planet.

There are often one or two moments in everyone's life where your understanding of things is challenged so heavily that you have to consider your own self and your own history to convince yourself you haven't gone crazy. Sometimes these moments are fleeting, almost troubling in their swiftness. Other times, times like this, they were so deeply and horrifyingly discomforting that you could become convinced that you would likely never recover.

I was staring down at Earth. It wasn't just similar or familiar, like in how something in life reminds you of a dream, or how you remember something from a memory but it's foggy and unconvincing. No.

This planet was identical.

The continents were all in their rightful places, the azure oceans were the exact same ones that I had often studied longingly from orbit in the past. The familiar mountain peaks rose high into the sky as they always had, and the deep green valleys sat nestled in their longtime homes.

I could feel my eyes darting across the blue and green surface, searching for something, something even remotely different, like the universe's hardest spot-the-difference puzzle.

"No no no no." The radio madness that flowed from my speakers washed over me and I began to drown in the staggering, paralyzing weight I suddenly felt. "This isn't right. This isn't—no, this just can't be right. There's no way. I—"

I opened a terminal window on a screen to my left and fought through the shake in my hands to bring up my ship's mission telemetry. I wanted nothing more in that moment than for that computer to tell me I had hallucinated the entire trip and that I was still back home, just now getting ready to leave.

KILOMETERS TRAVELLED: 3.4×10^{13} km

TIME OF TRIP (MISSION-RELATIVE): 2.625 years

TIME OF TRIP (EARTH-RELATIVE): 4.375 years

MISSION PROGRESS: 49%

Oh boy. I'd been to space almost a dozen times, but this was the first time I had ever felt truly nauseous. I checked again, and again, but every time it said the same thing. There was no doubt that I had travelled through the cosmos.

A yellow light began blinking above my head. My body stiffened up when I realized what it was for. It was the ship's comm light, alerting me to an incoming active communication. I don't know for how long, but I know I sat there and stared at that light. I had come this far. No sense chickening out now.

I shut off the wideband receiver. I couldn't decide what was more disconcerting, the impossible radio static or the immense silence that now filled the ship. I reached up and flicked the comms back on. A voice crackled through.

"Commander?"

"Yes?" I responded back, trying my best to cover up the anxiety I was feeling.

"It's been a long time," the voice said. It was quiet and a little more strained than I remembered, but it was undeniably familiar. There was no doubt who the voice belonged to. It was the Flight Director.

"I...uh, I—" *What the hell do I even say? What the hell is happening?* "Hi...how long has it been?" I asked.

"Almost nine years, Commander. I came out of retirement for this," she said, her voice hopeful and excited. "I wanted to be the one to welcome you back."

"Back?" The word slipped out.

"Yes...back home. It's been a long journey I can imagine."

"Well...not as long as you'd think."

"You have a planet full of people excited to hear

all about it," the Flight Director said. There was a pause and the Hermes was once again filled with a daunting silence. I felt as though I should say something, like I should ask any of the million questions that I had, or to try to explain *anything*, but the Flight Directors voice returned before I could decide. "Welcome home," she said softly, as if she was speaking just to me.

Unbound, Unchained

What is your *now*?

Most of you would say that it's the moment in the universe that you currently inhabit, the immediate instance in time that you're experiencing. Within those instances of *now* are the seemingly tangible set of references you have to justify what is *past*, *present*, and *future*. The world around you changes. Life grows and decays, things move from here to there, the air shifts. It's within those changes, however subtle, that you define *now*.

Now remove those earthly evolutions. Pull yourself away from the shifting amalgam of life, death, the minutiae of your own experiences.

Picture an expansion. Imagine a vast recess of black, empty space. There is no light, no matter, no material-you. It is only your consciousness and a massive void of quiet, beautiful nothingness. Does time still exist here for you? Does, or can, it exist without objects to fill it up, without reference? In this frame, does time still move from one point to the next, or is it just a fabric that you hang upon its infinite walls to explain away what you cannot?

In this space, each moment is the same as the one before it. It's the same as the next. There is no then, now, or later. There just *is*. In this reality, time fails to exist as a concept.

Maybe I'm speaking too much in the abstract, but the reality of time is a hard concept to grasp for someone like yourself. It's not that you're unintelligent or inept, by any means, in fact you've come a long way in so few years. It's that time is not some defining law of the universe. It's not a structured pathway for you to meander down for eternity. It simply exists as an explanation, a belief that allows you to comprehend the Universe.

How does one truly explain away a belief without defiling it?

Perhaps in terms you might understand.

You consider time to be linear.

We know it is not.

For you, time goes from the past to the future, and *now* is the in-between, the present experience as each moment passes on to the next. For you, there is only forward. No deviation, no return trip. And as such, you're afraid of it. You fear its passage because you cannot control its perceived effects on your life.

There is no such fear for us. We are not bound in

such irrational slavery to our own minds. We have long since won the freedom from those shackles. We toiled for millennia to break our self-imposed chains, but you've simply not fought hard enough. Your narrow outlook binds you to your fear of your past mistakes. That's not to say the fear isn't justified, no. If we lived as you do, we'd share your worry, your trepidation.

Time has been kind to us, though. She was once our master, but now we are freed.

You'll get there one day. I have faith you will. You'll put aside your war and strife, your ignorance, your inherent distaste for one another. You'll have no choice. Your species…it's on the precipice now. The end grows near. It's the cliff at the end of the tracks, and it's approaching fast.

You'll change or you'll die. Quite often it takes a catastrophe to open one's mind. Life is not without suffering, and with suffering comes clear headedness, but you'll soon be passed that. We were where you are now —fighting, hating, killing—because we feared a lack of it would lead to quiet. And quiet is the most terrifying thing of all when your time is limited. The thought of being alone with ourselves scares us more than anything, to have to live with the choices we've made without the ability to change them. It paralyzes you now, as it once did us.

From life to death we moved, and we longed to fill the in-between with as much as we could to make us feel alive. But feeling *alive* is not the same as *living*.

Living consists of those moments in between. But being *alive* is hard to describe. It's those moments, not those in between birth and death, but those that allow us to differentiate ourselves from our beginning and end.

Maybe one day you'll understand. You'll look back on this and understand what I mean. You'll empathize with your fellow kind, because you'll be able to reach out and touch their pasts. You'll be able to see all of them, then, now, and later. They will no longer be others to you, because you'll be able to experience all of what they are in this universe, from their inception to their eventual return to the cosmos, in an instance.

You'd be amazed how limiting *now* truly is. Most of you would say that it's the moment in the universe that you currently inhabit, but eventually, *now* will fall from your vocabulary. It will just be a thought on the distant horizons of your evolution, and it will be in that moment, the *here* and *then* of that reality, that we will finally meet.

The Disappearance of Casey Flack

"You hear from that guy?" Jack asked.

"Yeah, he didn't know anything." I responded back.

"Damn, a dead end then?"

"Yeah, another one."

"I just don't get it."

"Join the club. How does a girl just disappear?"

"I really think it had to be someone close to her...the uncle-"

"Nah, he had a legitimate alibi," I said, shaking my head.

"Christ...and those cameras caught nothing right?"

"You saw 'em yourself. Nothing. She was seen at the ATM, she walked towards the exit, but she was never seen coming out. I've gone over it a million times. No witnesses, no one's come forward..."

"No body parts mailed to her parents..."

"Come on, Jack, really?"

"Well, it's true! At least that would have given us something." He shrugged.

I stepped back from the board. The web of connecting diagrams, images, and text sprawled out wildly from the center image of a teenage girl. I leaned against my desk and took it all in. Jack sighed loudly and sat down behind his desk.

"This stuff tastes like shit," he said between sips of his cold coffee. "Blegh."

"We need to go back," I said while pulling my jacket on.

"Back? Where? Back to where she disappeared? What more is there to find, Jen?"

"Humor me." He did.

We went back to the location of her disappearance, the ATM. It was late afternoon and we were beginning to lose the daylight. Since her disappearance a few weeks ago, we hadn't found a shred of evidence at the ATM. We had only managed to pull a few complete prints off of the machine and the handle of the door leading in and out of the ATM, but none had led anywhere. Nothing had been found otherwise. No blood, no scuff marks. Jack shit.

"What are we looking for here, Jen? Jennifer?"

"Sorry, I just...there has to be something!" I was

tired. Very, very tired. Few cases in my career as a detective had so intensely frustrated and confused me.

"Look...I'm sorry but I just don't know how we can possibly find her. We've been at this for weeks and have gotten nowhere." He walked back towards the car. "She might as well have been taken by the Loch Ness Monster."

I followed with a sigh. I opened the driver-side door and hunched to get into the car when I noticed a small boy standing in the growing darkness a few feet from the ATM's door. He was maybe eight years old. He stared at me nervously, clearly unsure if he should approach.

"Wait wait, hold on, Jack. There's a kid."

"A kid? So?"

"Looks like he wants to talk to us. Doesn't he?" I stood back up and closed the car door. I walked over to the boy who, despite the anxious look on his face, stepped forward as I approached. I crouched to his height.

"Hi there," I said. "What's your name?"

"Mac," he said with a high-pitched, crackly voice.

"It's nice to meet you, Mac. You live around here?" He nodded. "You heard about the girl that went missing from here, right?" He nodded again, and I could tell by the sheepish look on his face that he hadn't simply heard about it on the news. "Have you been waiting around here hoping we'd come back?" He looked at me shyly for a few moments but eventually nodded. "Mac...were you here when the girl went missing?" Again, he took a little before responding. He looked over at Jack, who was now standing next to the car with his arms crossed and a skeptical look across his face. "Don't worry, he's a friend. Harmless really." I leaned in closer. "Between you and me, he's a big teddy bear, but don't tell him I said that. Shhhhh." Mac chuckled. "Were you here, Mac? When the girl disappeared?" I asked again. He nodded.

"Yep," he said quietly. I could feel my body tighten up and my stomach churn. It was the first witness, the first anything, since we had started working on the case.

"Did you see what happened? Was she taken? Did someone take her away?"

"Yeah."

I hadn't realized but Jack had moved closer and was now standing behind me, listening intently with a notepad in hand.

"Where did they take her?" Mac shook his head. "You don't know?" He nodded. "Who took her? What did they look like?" I reached back and tapped Jack's leg.

"I'm getting it all," he whispered back. I watched Mac shift in his stance and think for a moment before responding.

"He was, um, wearin' black, like um a jacket or somethin'—it had a hood and buttons." I could hear

Jack's pen scratching across the paper. "He was tall."

"Tall like me or tall like Jack?" I asked, motioning to Jack as I stood up next to him for comparison.

"In between," he said after viewing us up and down. I crouched back down.

"Did you see his face?"

He shook his head again. "No," he said, "sorry." His gaze fell towards the ground like he was in trouble.

"Hey, it's okay, you're being a big help!" I said loudly aimed both at Mac and Jack who caught my drift and cut in dryly with a "Yeah, pal, doing great." Mac smiled and looked back up at me.

"But, um, I did see that he had been hangin' around here a bit before. I was waitin' for my mom, who was in the store buying um, some stuff, I don't know, like girl stuff and juice and things. I didn't wanna go in because I get bored and she says that it's okay if I stand outside because she can see me through the windows, and, oh yeah, she was also buyin' cereal for me and my little sister, because we like the kind with the purple and blue marshmallows even though mom says they aren't good for us but we don't like that other kind so—"

"Mac, hold on, what do you mean he was hanging around here?"

"I saw him standin' around while I was waitin'."

"Around here?" I asked, gesturing to the area around the ATM. He nodded. I looked up towards a bank of angled security cameras. We had watched the recorded feed countless times, but, with so many people coming and going all day long, it was seemingly pointless and overly time consuming to fully investigate each one. Now we had something to go off.

"And you saw him take her, but didn't see where they went?" I asked. He nodded again. I looked up at Jack and he looked back quizzically with a raised eyebrow. "No idea which direction they went? This way? That way?" Mac just shrugged.

"I dunno. I saw 'em, then they were gone."

"Hmm, okay. Is there anything else you want to tell us?" I looked at him intently, hoping for one last breadcrumb to follow.

"Well, my mom once tried to make my little sister and I eat that cereal with the fruit in it but—"

"About the girl or the man that took her..." I interrupted. He shook his head. "Okay, thank you. You have been very, very helpful. This might help save this girl, Mac." I knew this very well may have been a lie, but it made him feel good, which was apparent by his huge smile. "You need a ride home? Are you out here alone?"

"No, my mom's in the store, buyin' some stuff, hopefully snacks."

We waved as we pulled away. He waved back excitedly.

"Alright, I've got the feed up from that day," Jack said.

"Okay, go about an hour before she was seen in

the ATM." He shifted the video back and we watched as the world went through a speedy reverse until he reached the requested time. "Play it. This guy has to be here somewhere." The minutes passed as did the passersby in the video. Some came and went down the sidewalk, in and out of the store that Mac's mom so commonly frequented, some in and out of the ATM. Minutes seemed to pass without any trace.

Then, a sudden glitch shifted and crackled and distorted the image. It lasted only a second or two, but, as it dissipated, a man in a black leather jacket could be seen standing clearly within the center of the frame.

"Holy crap, that's him," Jack said, disbelieving that the kid had actually told us the truth. The distortion had seemingly covered his entrance into the frame, and after a few minutes of him simply standing and looking around, he walked towards the ATM but then out of frame completely.

"Wait, where did he go? Find him, Jack!" He shifted between each of the feeds, but he wasn't anywhere. He had somehow disappeared between them. We tracked forward to the point at which the girl was last seen in the ATM, but there was no man in black.

"Maybe there's a blind spot somehow? The kid said he saw this guy grab and take her." Jack looked at me like I had answers, but I just shrugged and shook my head in disbelief.

"Well, we get a good look at his face here," I said as I rolled back the video and tapped my finger against the screen. "Let's run some facial scans and see if we get an I.D."

The scans took a while as the system ran the image through all of the databases that we had access to in the department. A series of beeps signified its completion, and I crossed my fingers as I walked back to Jack's computer to see what it had found.

Doug Hornbeck. Lived right outside the city. Seemed way too easy.

"We can't just bust into this guy's house," I commented. "We don't have any physical evidence against him. Mac's words and some sketchiness on a security camera won't go very far in court."

Jack nodded. "Yeah, but we can always pay him a visit? See if he knows anything?"

Doug Hornbeck's house was quaint, the sort of place you'd expect a middle aged, single guy to live. Flower pots lined his front porch, although most of the plants looked like they hadn't been watered in a while. The house appeared cared for but in a way that was almost out of necessity rather than for aesthetics. We pulled into the small driveway and parked behind an older black sedan. Someone was home.

I unsnapped the clasp on the top of my holster as I got out and kept my right hand firmly at the ready on top of the sidearm. We walked up the short set of stone steps to the bright blue front door.

"Alright, let's see who's home." I knocked a few

times on the door and almost immediately heard motion from inside. Steps and then an unlocking of the inner lock.

A portly man, partially balding on top and wearing a mustard yellow button-down shirt tucked into his faded grey pleated pants, answered the door. "Hello? How can I help you two today?" he questioned softly and with a warm smile.

"Mr. Hornbeck?" Jack asked.

"Yessir. And you?"

"Detective Crosby, and this is Detective Huang," Jack replied. "Do you mind if we come in, Mr. Hornbeck? Few questions for you regarding a missing persons case we're working on. Hoped you could help us out." The look on Doug's face shifted from warm and bright to concern, and I could see a legitimate air of confusion in his darting eyes and furrowed brow.

"Uh, yes, of course, officers. Please, come on in," he said, stepping aside and waving us in. "You'll have to excuse the mess, though. I've been doing some rearranging so everything's, well, all over the place." He wasn't wrong. As if his small home wasn't cramped enough, a mess of furniture and knick-knacks filled much of the already minimal open space. He waddled quickly into his living room and cleared a space off of an old, worn couch for Jack and me. He gestured for us to sit and we did. "Can I get you two anything to drink? Water, milk? I think maybe I have some cran-apple juice left?"

"No, thank you," we said in unison. It had taken me a few minutes, but it was clear. This man was definitely the one from the security camera footage. He seemed...rounder...and certainly less intense than the man in the video, but there was no question. It was unmistakably him.

He came back a few moments later with a short glass of water for himself and took a seat in a large cushy chair across from us. His jolly disposition had returned in full, although he looked at us expectantly. I took that as my cue.

"Mr. Hornbeck," I said, "as my partner mentioned, we're working on a missing persons case. I want to preface this now by saying that, as of this moment, you are not being considered a suspect and are not being charged with anything." The first part wasn't exactly entirely truthful, but you have to lead with something convincing. "You appeared in CCTV footage in the area around the time of the supposed abduction of the victim." His eyes narrowed as I spoke, but he otherwise reacted little. "We're just following up with the pedestrians who we could identify in the video to see if we could work out any additional information that might be helpful." He nodded in understanding.

"Well of course I'll help how I can." I could see Jack out of the corner of my eye and I knew he was doing his best to read the man sitting across from us.

"Are you familiar with the First National ATM on the corner of Waltham Street and East Lorelai, sir?"

He thought for a moment. "Yes, I believe so," he said, pausing for a moment more, then, "yes, yes I do," he confirmed confidently. "I can't say I frequent that ATM very often—I have a different bank, not great but some good interest rates—but there is a nice cafe around the corner that I visit every once in a while. Great coffee." He added with a smile. I scribbled his response into my notes.

"And, if you can recall, were you near that ATM on Monday, July 18th around 4 p.m.?" This time his response was much quicker.

"No, I wasn't. I always work until five." I looked over at Jack, who looked back with a quizzical look on his face that was hopefully far subtler to Doug than it was to me. I thought for a moment before starting on a new line of questioning.

"What do you do for work, Mr. Hornbeck?"

"I'm an actuary."

"An actuary?" Jack asked, speaking for the first time since we had sat down and sounding more confused than I had expected.

"Yes, I compile and analyze statistics and use them to calculate insurance risk—"

"Yeah, I know what it is," Jack responded back sharply. Doug's face crinkled into a look of consternation but unfurled it just as fast.

"And would your work be able to confirm your location on that date and time for us if we reached out to them?" I asked.

"I'm quite sure they could, Detective. Much of the office is still there at that time, so there are quite a few who could confirm that for you," he responded back plainly. I began to make a note to contact his employers, but I decided against it. There was no point.

He sipped at his water sheepishly as Jack and I stared at him across the messy room. I had been a detective for a long time, and I had been a street cop before that. I had spoken to a lot of perps, a lot of suspects, a lot of innocent people and a lot of truly guilty people. You had to be good at reading people in this job, and I was good at reading people. It's one of the things that made me a good detective. But sitting across from this man right now, it was obvious...he wasn't guilty. I could tell that Jack agreed by the way he shifted anxiously next to me. There was always a fairly foolproof way to tell, though, and it was the only thing left I could think to try.

"Casey Flack," I said slowly. I watched him as the words left my mouth. No response, verbal or physical. "Have you ever heard that name, Mr. Hornbeck?"

He sat back and scrunched his lips up as he pondered the name. "No, I don't believe so."

"Maybe a client of yours? Someone you've calculated risk for, perhaps?"

"Is she the owner of a local business, by chance?" He asked back. Now I was the confused one.

"No, sir. She's 16," I responded. He shrugged

with a *that-answers-that* look on his face.

"Then no. Our only clients are local businesses." He was telling the truth. Jack had clearly heard enough. He stood and I followed. Doug stood abruptly in response.

"That all, detectives? Anything more I can do to help?"

"That'll be all, Mr. Hornbeck. Thank you for your help," I said as we turned and walked back towards the front door. He handed us a business card as we left, but I knew we wouldn't be needing it. He was innocent.

The next few weeks were more of the same. Dead ends and a lot of "I don't know"s. I had quickly grown tired of having to tell her parents that we still didn't have anything to go on. It was exhausting.

The kid's story never really went anywhere. He said he had seen Doug Hornbeck actually abduct Casey, but no one else did. There was no doubt that Doug Hornbeck had appeared in the security camera footage, but every other aspect of our conversation with him convinced us that he was telling us the truth that he had no clue who Casey Flack was, and he really believed that he had been at work when the abduction occurred. We did end up contacting his work, and they confirmed as much, that, as far as anyone could remember, he was in the office. For all we knew, he had taken a short trip for an afternoon coffee. Regardless, we kept an APB circulating throughout local departments just in case someone caught him doing something suspicious. Unlikely.

"Wanna grab a bite to eat, Jen?" Jack asked as he put on his jacket. His question pulled me sharply from thought and it was only then that I realized how dark it was outside.

"Why not?" I said. "I'm feelin' shawarma. Shawarma good?"

"The hell is shawarma?" He asked.

I chuckled. "I honestly don't know. It's good though!" We made it most of the way to the door before the phone on my desk rang.

"Oh come on, it's quitting time," Jack remarked with a sigh. Normally, considering the time, I would have agreed and ignored it, but I didn't. I don't know why...maybe it was the desperate hope that it was something useful. I jogged briskly back towards my desk and he remained in the doorway.

"Detective Huang," I greeted into the old black handset.

"Detective, this is Officer Haskins from the 6th precinct. We just got a call about that guy you put the BOLO out for. Name is..." the officer paused, and I could hear shifting paper on the other end.

"Doug Hornbeck?" I interjected desperately.

"Ah yes, thank you, yeah him," the officer confirmed. "Showed up in the same black clothing again. We've got officers standing at the ready."

"Where?"

Our car flew down the dark roads. I could barely hear the constant radio chatter of updates from the officers on the scene over the sound of the wind blasting against the car. I kept rubbing my sweaty palms against my pant legs.

"Faster, Jack," I commanded.

"Can't, Jen. Can't catch him if we don't make it there alive."

I was still adamantly confused about how Doug Hornbeck was involved. Very little, if anything at all, about our conversation led me to believe he was, but it was all we had. He was either an incredible liar, or a psychopath, or maybe both.

I alerted the officers who were waiting at a safe distance that we were almost there, and a *copy* crackled back in return.

We pulled up some blocks away. An officer on the scene pointed Hornbeck out from a distance. He was leaning against a cement wall between a bakery and a department store. He glanced up and around every once in a while, before returning his gaze back down towards something on his wrist.

"Now or nothing. You good?" Jack asked.

"Let's do it."

We walked out into the street and towards the sidewalk where Doug was standing. Just like in the video, he seemed different. It was definitely him, but he was thinner and far more hardened looking than the feeble, nervous man we met.

"Doug Hornbeck!?" I shouted as we grew close. He looked up immediately and we made eye contact. Something wasn't right. It hit me in the split second we locked eyes, but before I could say anything to Jack, Hornbeck lunged from the wall and began a full sprint down the street.

"Shit," Jack huffed as he began a labored run in pursuit, his large build and paunch swaying heavily side to side with each step.

"I'll cut him off!" I yelled back to him as I cut between two buildings in the hope that I could get on the other side quickly. I sprinted down a long alley filled with dumpsters and refuse. I couldn't help but scrunch my face in response to the smell, but I pushed past it and to the other side. I turned hard down another alley, this one behind a set of apartment buildings, and then continued again down another. I realized I could hear Hornbeck's steps and his heavy breathing as I neared the end of the third alley. I found an opening between two of the buildings that led back out to the main street and waited. His labored breaths grew louder. I could hear Jack behind him, yelling expletives between shouts of "get back here!" and "stop running!" Finally, he grew close enough and I pounced from behind my wall.

I wrapped my arms tight around his waist as we collided with the ground. He wriggled in an attempt to break free, but I had him. I spun him around and pushed his face hard into the ground as I pulled his arms behind his back and snapped on a pair of handcuffs.

"Why were you running, Doug?" I asked between tight breathes

"How do you know who I am?" He asked.

"We met you the other day, dipshit," Jack said. I hadn't realized he had caught up, but I was glad he was there. "You forget already? Why were you running?" He kept shifting, fighting my weight against his back, but he didn't answer the question.

"Something's wrong, Jack. It's, well it's him, but it's not," I said. He radioed in for a squad car but after a few moments he nodded in agreement.

"Yeah, he moved pretty quick for a portly little guy," he commented. "As a matter of fact, he ain't so portly anymore." You could tell, even through the thick, baggy clothes, that this man was far more fit than the one we had spoken to.

"Did you kidnap Casey Flack? What have you done with her?" Again, nothing but muffled grunts. "Were you going to kidnap someone else today? Who were you looking for?" A glint of light from his wrist caught my attention as he shifted aggressively underneath me. It wasn't a watch so much as a small computer. It had an assortment of buttons that looked like they belonged in the 80's, yet the screen at the center, which was filled with brightly colored numbers and constantly shifting geometry, looked far more advanced. I yanked at the strap so that it came loose and fell to the ground. "What is this?" I asked as I held the device near his face.

"Nothing you'd understand." His voice was gruff, strained, and couldn't have sounded more unlike the meek man we had met. Jack's radio came in loud, a mix of chatter both intense and impatient. I looked up at him curious to the sudden outburst of communication, but he raised an *I'll handle it* finger into the air and then walked some distance away. I could hear his "calm down calm down" as he answered the calls. The sirens of the squad cars filled the air as they turned onto the street.

"Look, Doug, you have got to give us something. It'll get a lot harder for you if you don't."

His struggle slowed suddenly. I could feel his body go limp under my weight. I flipped him and watched as foam spilled from his mouth and his eyes whitened and began to roll back in his head. He must have had a hidden cyanide capsule in one of his teeth. "Oh, shit. No no, please no!" I yelled at the now fully unresponsive body beneath me. A swarm of officers ran up to me and pushed me off as they began CPR on the clearly deceased Doug Hornbeck.

Was he so afraid of prison, of us, that he would have rather killed himself? Maybe it was simply a means of protecting something...some sort of information so important that he would rather die than have us know.

I could feel my skin grow hot and flustered. I placed my hands tight against the back of my neck. What the hell would we do now? On cue, I could hear

Jack yelling for me and running, or as much as he could call running, towards me.

"Jen!" He struggled out of breath. "You are not going to beli-believe it."

"I very well might after today."

"Casey Flack..." he paused, unsure of how to justify his own words, "...she just walked into the station."

The girl, looking far younger than she actually was, sat deflated in the chair. Her clothing was dirty and torn and her shirt draped off of her shoulder on one side. She stared down at the ground, only looking up periodically as she answered one question or another. The water vapor rising from the cup of hot coffee that she held in her hands flitted through the air and shifted with each of her heavy, slow breaths.

"And you don't know where he brought you?" I asked.

"It was in some warehouse, I don't know. He bound me, so I couldn't see until we got there."

"But it was local? If you had to guess?" She seemed to ponder that question.

"Yes...and no, I don't know."

"What do you mean by yes and no?" Jack asked.

"Well, it was far, but it wasn't. It was like we had gone away somewhere far, but it wasn't really. It was still here," she said, gesturing in a wide arc above her head as she said *here*.

"Here? As in the police station?" Jack tried to clarify.

"No no, here as in this, I don't know, place. Where we are, but not actually where we are." I could tell in her eyes that she wasn't crazy. What she was saying was her truth.

"Casey...how did you escape?" I asked her, hoping for something clearer. Instead, she looked up at me earnestly and then reached into a deep, almost hidden pocket that lined the side of her baggy pants.

"With this," she said, handing me the device that Doug had been wearing on his wrist when we caught him. Except this wasn't the same one. That one was sitting in evidence. This was another of the same type. "I managed to steal it off of him."

I held it in my hand. With a tap, the screen came alive and filled itself with numbers and graphs and shapes that shifted and changed and grew and shrunk.

I stood up and looked at Jack, who was staring back at me incredulously. "Call Doug Hornbeck's house, Jack." His face changed from disbelief to utter confusion.

"You watched him die, Jennifer. No one is home to answer that phone."

"Sure there is. Doug Hornbeck is home," I said plainly. "*Our* Doug Hornbeck."

The End of the End of Us as We Know It

You'd be hard-pressed to find someone who hasn't, at least at some point in their life, thought about the *end*. Not as in *we all grow old and die so be nice to people and don't forget to feed your cat in the meantime*, but more like the *end of times*. You know, the apocalypse, Judgement Day, Armageddon (not to be confused with the dumb but shamefully enjoyable movie where Ben Affleck plays with animal crackers to the tune of Aerosmith's "I Don't Want to Miss a Thing"). It's just one of those existential things that has plagued humanity for as long as humanity has been a thing.

Quite honestly, there has always been a pretty good business in end-of-the-world prophecies. Christians had The Rapture, the Norse had Ragnarok, the Mayans had 2012 (again, I mean the year, not the movie), the list goes on. The manner in which the end actually occurs varies from culture to culture and from apocalyptic story to apocalyptic story, but in the end, the capital-E end always happens.

Let me be clear: the world did end. I'll preface this story, though, with "it didn't happen any of the ways anyone expected." Or at least, it didn't happen *exactly* how anyone predicted. Sure, we were invaded by aliens, and so the "End is Nigh! Aliens walk among us!" guys were sort of right. But no one could have possibly predicted the strange, awful, just really and truly terrible things that happened at the end.

Although, you're probably asking yourself, "but wait, thus-far-nameless narrator, the world couldn't have actually ended, because you're alive to tell us about it, right?" Well, yeah, okay, valid point. Our planet is still, mostly, in one piece, and it's still in orbit around its star, and it's still technically churning along like it always has been. There are still living animals and people and stuff. But let's be honest, it's about as close a world-ending cataclysm as most people will likely ever experience. And calling it the "end of the world" just sounds so much better than "sort of the end of most of the world kind of." This isn't really a story about *how* it happened, though. Instead, I'd like to tell you about why the invasion of the Arachnids sucked as much as it did.

It's not because most of the world's population was wiped out in the ensuing war. Also not because the planet was left a mostly desolate wasteland. It sucked because now I have to walk five *dangerous* miles—through The Alley and Hawk gang-territory—to buy toilet paper. "Why go through so much danger and effort to buy toilet paper?" you ask. Well, the apocalypse is bad enough, why make your ass suffer as well?

It was a trip I had often made. Mind you, it was not exclusively for teepee. No, the small market where my seller was located contained other assorted commodities. Band aids, goggles, those little snack cake things with the striped frosting on them and the cream on the inside...you know, the essentials.

I found myself especially unmotivated for one particular trip. Racky sightings had been up the previous few weeks in The Alley and I was in no mood to deal with that. On this particular occasion, though, the trip was unusually necessary.

Thankfully, the acid rain stayed at bay that day and I was able to walk freely out in the open without my uncomfortable vacsuit.

I trudged from my abode and out of the maze of buildings it resided in. The world opened into a large crossing. Left was the bridge that spanned across the massive river that ran alongside our once impressive city. Right led deeper into the city towards the no-go zone. Straight led directly into The Alley.

The Alley was an almost five mile stretch of road that ran parallel to the river. It used to be an important, lively street before the invasion. Now, it's often considered a death sentence. That was, of course, unless you knew the right way.

Spoiler alert: I knew the right way.

The Alley was lined on both sides by tall, almost aggressively intrusive buildings. The steel beams, broken structures, and stone outcroppings that had since fallen from their edifices bordered the main road through The Alley, creating natural choke points and barricades. Obstacles to most, these proved not only beneficial, but deeply advantageous to the primary residents of The Alley, the Hawks (arrogantly named for their avian namesake's supposed arachnid-killing talents). In reality, there were very few rackies left because they had been mostly annihilated, along with the majority of the human race, during the war that followed their invasion. The Hawks, ever haughty in their opinions of themselves, spread the narrative that they themselves had wiped the majority of rackies from existence and would continue to do so as long as any remain.

Not that they're very easy to find anymore. Very few of the remaining Arachnids still exist in their original forms. Turns out that they have this technology that allows them to transfer their consciousness into another living thing. As humans arguably have the most similar bodies to their own, we were typically the vessels of choice. Lucky for us (I guess?), the process is apparently incredibly difficult. It's also permanent. I'd be lying if I said that there were no world leaders during the war that suddenly launched nuclear warheads against their own people or military commanders who suddenly shot themselves in the head, but the invaders mostly remained in their own bodies.

This changed as the war came to an end. With no way home and a perhaps unsurprisingly massive target on their heads, most of the remaining rackies zapped themselves into humans and hoped it would be enough to blend in and live out the rest of their days in peace. That's why the recent increase in sightings of rackies in their original bodies had been so surprising. They had been seen regularly along The Alley and in the surrounding areas as if searching for something. Whatever the reasons, it must have been important, because they were bringing immense danger to themselves in looking for it.

I don't blame them for wanting to hide. How could you? They were hunted day and night. Sure, they did some pretty bad stuff, but they weren't all bad in my experience. Some of them were good.

I thought about it as I made my way along my typical route through The Alley. The Geiger counter strapped to my belt vibrated lightly as it picked up radioactive emissions from the no-go zone to my right. Despite being within spitting distance of a fairly massive amount of radioactive fallout, this was still safer than taking the main road or sticking closer to the river. I had taken the river route once. Never again. Let's just say I went home bloody and with no toilet paper.

One could only hope in the five-mile trip that you'd see neither a person nor an alien. On this particular day, I was not so lucky.

I was barely 30 minutes in, just about a third of the way to the other side of The Alley, when I ran into my first real obstacle. Actually, it was more like a dozen obstacles. Through a massive wall of glass windows, I could see a group of Hawks gathered around a pile of rubble inside what used to be the lobby of some office building. Unusual. This building wasn't typically frequented or used by the gang. They were here and gathered for a specific reason.

I considered turning back to try to circle around, but it would have brought me much closer to the main road and more directly through territory that I knew the Hawks regularly patrolled. I could stray a little into the no-go zone by going around the building completely, but there was no guarantee how long I'd need to do that, and I had run out of radiation sickness meds weeks ago. Despite the clear stupidity in continuing forward, trying to sneak past them was likely still the safest, and quickest, path forward.

I crawled through a buckled section of the building's outer wall. I was deposited into what used to be a women's bathroom. This bathroom gave me the creeps every time I passed through it. Inside the middle stall, whose door had long since been torn from its hinges, a now darkened and dried splatter of blood marked the wall above the toilet. A bullet hole in the center of the splatter told enough of a story. I'd never seen the body and I didn't know the person, but I always tried to move quickly by the stall. In the almost 10 years since the beginning of the war, I had seen horrible, horrible things. But this, this just made me feel a deep, resounding sadness.

I continued out of the bathroom into a short hallway that led directly into the lobby. The Hawks were all still standing around chatting, and, while I couldn't hear what they were talking about, I could now see that they weren't just standing around a pile of rocks. They were, in fact, standing around a dead racky. The once shining metallic body was now covered in dirt and green fluid, its blood. I could tell by the dishevelment of some of the Hawks that they had killed it themselves.

Their mumbling was intense, quick, and some of them appeared to be arguing. I took the opportunity of distraction to attempt my sneak. I crawled up behind a half-wall in the back of the lobby and slowly moved along its length. I remained as close to the ground as I could without going prone in case I needed to make a run for it.

I had had previous run-ins with the Hawks countless times over the years. Clearly, I had survived the encounters, but not without a loss of belongings, blood, and dignity. They loved taking advantage of those willing to pass through their territory just as much, maybe even more, than they loved killing aliens. As such, they were, effectively, the toll keepers between the Market and anyone who lived opposite The Alley from it. Their toll varied, but it was always unreasonable. You provided supplies or blood. Sometimes both.

I had few supplies left, and I had already shed enough blood.

I moved as stealthily as I could manage. It became apparent, though, as I continued further along the wall, that I was running out of hiding space. The fight that had ensued between the Hawks and the racky had clearly broken through a massive middle section of my cover. I'd now have to cross a 15-foot gap entirely uncovered and well within sight of at least a few of the Hawks.

I made it as far along the cover as I could until I reached the gap. I found a suitably-sized chunk of the rubble and lobbed up in a high arc over the wall and past the group of waiting gang members. It clacked against the ground beyond them.

"You hear that?" one of them asked the group.

"Yeah, man, from over there," another said. I peeked over my cover to confirm their attention had been drawn away. Satisfied it had, I began my quiet crossing across the gap. I made it three quarters of the way when I heard a voice, louder and far closer than the others.

"Look who it is! Look guys, it's Will!" Oh shit. I froze in place. "You trying to hide from us, friend?" The voice said again. "That's not very nice."

"Hey Kai, what's up?" I asked, trying to mask the horrible annoyance that was rippling through my body.

"Where you off to on this fine day?" He asked flippantly as his colleagues began to circle up around us. "I liked your little attempt," he said, motioning in the direction of where my rock had landed.

"Yeah...sorry about that. In a bit of a rush today," I said with a shrug.

"So much of a rush you didn't even want to say hi to your friends?" His crooked, scarred smile showcased a set of large, browned teeth. I knew the false pleasantries would give way to demand soon, and I had little to give him that they would find acceptable. I was nervous he wouldn't like what he found if he patted me down. Let's just cut to the chase and get this over with. I had shit to do.

"Hey, man, look...I don't have much for you," I said with my hands up in apology.

"Look at this guy," he remarked towards his underlings. "Cutting straight to business." The other Hawks laughed. It wasn't even funny. "Alright, Will," he waved me towards him. "Watcha got?"

"Not much, Kai," I said, shrugging my shoulders again like an idiot. He responded with a tsk tsk and walked the remaining few feet so that he was standing right in front of me.

"Come on, brother. You know the drill."

"Yeah, I know the drill." I nodded. *Alright, I guess this is going to happen.* I reached my hand back slowly towards my belt. The Hawks noticed and responded aggressively. They pulled out their weapons, a mixture of rifles, handguns, and sharpened machete-like things that I'm sure would hurt really bad if hit by one, and they aimed them quickly in my direction.

"Woah woah woah," shouted Kai. "You be careful there, Will. Ain't no one want to die today. I'm sure you agree." He pulled his own handgun up and aimed it at me.

"Calm down. It's chocolate," I said frustrated as I pulled a handful of chocolate bars from the pack attached to my belt. Kai looked at me up and down with a serious, strained face. We stood there in silence for a few moments. My butt cheeks were admittedly very sweaty. After a while, his constipated look gave way to a wiry chuckle and then a hearty laugh.

"Lower 'em, boys," he commanded. The Hawks lowered their weapons and the lobby became far less tense. I could feel my ass unclench. Kai reached forward to grab the candy. He eyed the bars for a moment and then he looked back at me with a shit-eating grin. He tore the plastic off of one and took a bite. He seemed to ponder the morsel a bit and then, satisfied, chewed it without mercy as he maintained long, horribly awkward eye contact with me.

"It's been a while. Just as good as I remember," he said.

"Good," I said dryly. I sounded more relieved than I intended, but oh well. "I'll let you fellows enjoy those." I turned quickly and began to leave. A heavy hand fell onto my shoulder and gripped tightly as it spun me around with a pull.

"Not so fast, friend. It's an appreciated donation," Kai said coolly, tossing the chocolate bars backwards into the arms of one of his buddies, "but it's not enough." He pushed down hard with the hand on my shoulder. I obliged and fell to my knees, because what the hell else was I going to do? I was horribly outnumbered and stood absolutely no chance.

"I feel like we've done this so many times, William, haven't we?" Kai holstered his handgun and reached his hand out sideways. One of his goons placed the handle of a metal baseball bat into his open palm. "I figured after all these times, after all these lessons we've taught you, you'd have learned. But you look down at us like we're thugs and savages." He wasn't wrong, and my admittedly brazen shrug of agreement clearly wasn't appreciated. His tone became frustrated and solemn. "We're not thugs, we're just...misunderstood. We're your protection, we look out for those of you who still remain. If we weren't around, who'd take care of all the bugs?" He asked it like a question, but I knew it was more of a statement, a falsely confident assessment of their own place in the new world.

"Come on, man," I said. "I don't want any of this bad guy end of the world shtick from you. You used to be an accountant." Hey, it's true, why not point it out? "Just get it over with so I can get on with my day." I tried my hardest to sound cool and confident, but I was scared. I had gotten these beatings before. Broken bones, days in bed. They weren't fun. "I have places to be." I couldn't tell if what I said made him angry or not, because his vicious smile never left. He stepped back and pulled the bat up over his head.

But holy deus ex machina am I lucky. Well, lucky-ish.

Something made a loud scuffling sound behind him as he brought the bat up into the air.

"Is there someone with you?" Kai asked impatiently. I shook my head sheepishly as I realized what was likely happening. There were few people confident enough to attack such a larger group of Hawks, but the owner of that sound wasn't a person. That's why I said "lucky-ish."

"Spread out, guys. There's someone around here. Find 'em."

The Hawks did as they were told, brandishing their weapons and breaking out to search the large lobby. It was cavernous in size, but there was fallen concrete and edifice everywhere, some of it piled into high mounds. Plenty of opportunities to sneak up if you had the confidence to do so.

Kai remained standing in front of me, and I stayed on my knees as he did so. He stared at me accusingly.

"Anything?" he shouted.

"Nothing," one of the Hawks responded.

"Where are they?" Kai asked me. "Make this easy." I just looked up at him. Thankfully, a pained scream from one of his men broke the tension. I watched him flinch but he remained focused on me.

"There's something here, boss," came a shout from deeper in the lobby.

"What? What's here?" he asked back.

A nervous-looking Hawk appeared from behind a large pile of rubble some 20 feet away. "I don't think it's with him, Kai," and with that a shining metal spike exploded through the front of the Hawk's face. His wriggling body was lifted into the air and then tossed hard aside. It went limp and lifeless as it hit the ground. A racky loomed tall behind where the Hawk stood moments prior. It rose about the height of your average professional basketball player. If you ignored the entirely metal body, the misshapen and uncanny facial features, and the eight long, horrifying, spindly appendages that protruded from its back, it looked fairly similar to a human. It walked primarily on two legs, had two main arms, and had similar, mostly human-like proportions.

It looked down at its fallen comrade that lay in a crumpled, bloodied pile a few feet away. Its gaze then shifted to myself and Kai.

"Told you," I said. "Not with me."

Another scream echoed through the large space and gunfire rang out. "Boss! Rackies!"

"No shit!" Kai yelled back. Without hesitation, he tossed the bat hard towards the Arachnid. It swatted it out of the air with one of its spindles, but it provided enough time for Kai to pull his gun and start to fire off rounds. The racky lunged quickly towards us. I didn't wait around to find out what would happen next.

I jolted up off the ground and threw myself backwards towards the half-wall I had originally hid behind. I vaulted over the wall and then sprinted full tilt in the direction I had originally been headed. To my left I could hear all kinds of sounds. Gunfire, metal hitting metal, the squelching of tearing flesh, and shouts of all kinds. I decided to let my imagination fill in the details. I threw my shoulder hard into the exit door at the end of the room and fell out the other side of the building.

I pulled myself off of the ground and ran blindly away from the building. If it wasn't for the sudden and aggressive vibrations against my hip, I would have run straight into the no-go zone. I readjusted towards the left but kept up pace. I straightened out as the vibrations from the Geiger counter lessened to a safe degree. I was being loud in my quick escape away from the building and I knew it was possible that I could run into more Hawks, but I would have preferred that over being skewered by a racky, so I kept going. The savage sounds from the building eventually became inaudible and I slowed my pace. I had covered a good distance and, assuming I kept to the shadows the rest of the way there, I was fairly confident that I was now safe from at least those back in the building who survived and decided I was worth the effort to search for.

Once I caught my breath and fell back into my normal route, I let my mind wander back towards the racky attack. It was odd in hindsight. Such a direct, even brutal, attack on a group of Hawks was bold. No single human was a match for a single racky, but a larger group of experienced humans could put up a fight against at least a few, so it was a risky assault. Maybe it was retribution for their fallen friend? Something more? I thought about it for a while before I realized I had almost arrived at the end of The Alley.

I exited out the side of a building and emerged into another large intersection. Much like the one on the other side of The Alley, one direction went across the river, although the bridge had collapsed a few years ago. The street to the right went into the no-go zone, and straight went right into The Market.

It was easier to feel a bit safer at this point since it was no longer technically Hawk territory, but it was important not to let your guard down. Just because there were fewer Hawks didn't mean the populace of The Market was any less dangerous.

Despite its name, The Market was less a gathering of shops and people doing friendly, professional business and more a fairly seedy group of mostly hidden individuals from which one could buy or trade things for other things. I had been so many times that I knew most of both the sellers and the patrons, and as such I had gained quite a rapport with many of them.

One such person was my toilet paper guy, Adam. Adam was a jolly fellow, far more likable than some of his colleagues, but I had always had a strange feeling about him, like he was hiding something dark underneath the rosy cheeks and warm welcomes. I had long heard rumors and stories from other regulars of the Market about Adam. They varied wildly from person to person, but most agreed that he used to have a wife and two children. He never talked about them, but I could only imagine he had likely lost them during the war.

But today, Adam was just as upbeat as usual.

"Will! Come in, pal, come in! It's good to see you." He threw up a massive trunk of an arm in greeting. "What brings you around today?"

"The usual," I said as I walked up towards his "counter." It was more of a pile of boxes, really, but it functioned the same.

"1-ply or 2-ply?" he asked.

"Am I a savage?" I retorted back with a scoff. He chuckled.

"Hey, man, I have to ask. You never know." He turned around and started rummaging through a series of high stacked containers. I stood there in silence for a few minutes as he searched through his stock.

"Adam," I said with a pause.

"What's up?" he responded, his back still turned to me.

"I was curious if you'd heard a specific rumor recently."

"A rumor?"

"Yeah. I heard a story the other day…apparently a racky in a skin suit has been kidnapped. You hear about it?"

He paused briefly to ponder my question. "I don't think so, man, sorry."

"Hmm, okay. I had heard that it had been kidnapped and was actually being held somewhere around here...in The Market actually."

"In The Market you say? Interesting."

"I'd say. I'd love to get my hands around that thing's throat. Squeeze the life out of it, yanno?" He paused his search once more as I stopped talking, but he continued after a few moments of silence. "So, you haven't heard about any of that? None of that rings a bell?"

"Nah, sorry, Will. Not ringing a bell." He cut himself off. "Ah, here we go! Sorry about that, they were underneath the Vienna sausages." He placed a small box of 2-ply toilet paper rolls on the "counter."

"It's no problem. What do I owe you?" I asked.

"You have copper?"

"A little."

"A few spools of that'll do."

"You got it." I reached behind me towards my pack. "You know, Adam...I don't think you're being entirely truthful with me."

"Excuse me?"

"I think you have heard about that kidnapped racky. I think you're lying to me." Adam's eyes widened, and he startled back as he noticed the handgun I had pulled from my belt. I had it pointed straight at his gut.

"In fact, I think you know exactly where it's being held."

"Woah, man. I don't know what you're going on about, b-but I have no clue, man. I don't know. What do you want me to do?" He asked, his voice higher in pitch than I was used to.

"I need you to open that door, Adam," I said as I motioned towards a door behind him that was mostly obscured by his stack of boxes. He looked back at me dumbfounded, but he could tell I wasn't bluffing. In reality, I honestly wasn't even sure if I was being totally serious or bluffing, but it only mattered that he believed me. He finally turned and began unstacking the boxes.

"You're going to kill it, right?" he asked nervously. "It's dangerous. It's a monster!" He looked back at me pleadingly. "You have to kill it."

I stared back at him coolly and he turned to finish unstacking. He pulled a bronze key from his pocket and, with one last, heavy sigh, unlocked and opened the door.

The small space was dark and damp. My eyes adjusted quickly and I noticed a pale, crumpled shape cowering in the corner. I moved slowly towards it and it recoiled.

"You okay?" I asked, kneeling down beside it.

A gaunt, dark haired woman stared up at me. She studied my face for a few moments. The sheer look of terror on her face shifted first to confusion and then to unquestionable relief. She nodded weakly.

I pulled the gag from her mouth and unwrapped the cloth that had been used to tie her wrists and ankles. "Can you stand?" With a little help she got onto her feet and, after a quick moment of self-calibration, nodded again. I threw her arm around my shoulder to provide some support and we exited the small space. I kept my gun trained on Adam as we made our way back through the small shop.

"You have to kill it! It's a killer, Will! If you don't kill it, that thing will kill you!" Unlike his typical jovial self, he sounded maniacal. We kept walking towards the door.

"This *thing's* name is Kato," I said. "She saved me." I didn't bother to look up at Adam's face, but I could feel his speechlessness as I spoke. "Just returning the favor."

I stopped as we got to the door and I began to turn the handle. "Oh crap, I almost forgot." I leaned Kato up against the door frame, she gave me a look of *go ahead I'm okay,* and I walked back towards Adam.

He looked horrified. At me, at her, at the situation. He shifted away from me as I grew closer. I shoved the gun back into my belt and reached into my pack. I pulled out a few small spools of copper wire and tossed them onto the counter. I grabbed the box of toilet paper and shoved it underneath my arm. "Almost forgot these," I said with a chuckle. "That would have been bad."

I nodded some thanks back in Adam's direction

and turned back towards the exit. Kato threw her arm
back around my shoulders and we exited through the
open door, closing it shut behind us.

Humanity

I: The Mountain

Our military Humvee moved quickly along the thin mountain pass. Snowdrifts on both sides narrowed the road down to a single lane, assuming it was anything more than that to start. The mountain face rose dozens of meters on our right and disappeared into the clouds above. On the left, there was nothing but a sheer drop into the foggy nothingness of the mountain valley below.

I was sitting in my office less than eight hours before. Now I was being rushed up a mountain thousands of miles away with a knot in my stomach and a deep uncertainty for what would come next. I was moving away from the solace of my life and the comfort in the fact that I could accept everything about it. My confidence in the world that I understood told me I would be fine, but some part of me fought against that with an anxiety that permeated through me as we made our way up the mountain.

"Doctor Hart. Doctor Hart, sir...we're almost at the site," said the uniformed NCO in the front passenger seat.

"Y-yes, okay, thank you, Sergeant Johnson." Odd. In the quickness with which I was retrieved and the chaos that ensued in getting here as fast as possible, I never got the Sergeant's name, yet it came to me quickly and with confidence. Strange, but the thought was quickly pushed from my mind given everything else occupying it. "What will happen when we're there?" I asked, partially shouting over the rumble of the V8s and the buffeting of the wind against the mountain.

"Sir? What do you mean what will happen?" he questioned back, eyeing the thin road.

"Well, I mean what happens next?" I knew he had understood my question the first time, but I'm not sure anyone in the truck, anyone on the mountain, or anyone around the world at this very moment knew how to answer. I suppose I'm not quite sure what I expected he would say. It was a dishearteningly difficult question given the circumstances, and, in all honesty, it wasn't even the one I really wanted answered. Vocalizing the real one would have been a waste because I'm sure we were all thinking it. *What do we do now that we know we're not alone?*

II: The Egg

As our convoy made its way up and over the final ridge, it quickly became clear that none of us were truly prepared for what was at the top. The mountain road suddenly gave way to a surprisingly large, flat clearing. The circular space was hidden from the road until breaching the hill at the top, so I was shocked at the sheer size when we entered. High cliff faces surrounded the area for half of its circumference. The remaining half dropped steeply into the valley below. The clearing was tucked away from the world, except for those who knew it was there. Perhaps it had once been buried beneath the mountain, uncovered by some long ago rock collapse or shift in the earth.

Brown military tents, hard-shell habitats, and vehicles filled the edges of the space. The "compound", for lack of a better word, had clearly been efficiently assembled and with an apparent urgency that seemed uncharacteristic even for the military. Uniformed officers and others, many of whom looked far above my pay grade, milled about busily.

Some of them were clearly taking the situation more in stride than others. Many of the military types went about their duties admirably stone-cold, while some did so with one hand nervously planted on their firearms. As we pulled up to a stop next to the largest of the three habitats, or habs, in the clearing, I watched as a man in an officer's uniform escorted a shaking man with wet eyes into a jeep.

In the center of the clearing, surrounded by orange barriers and a phalanx of troops, bureaucrats, and scientists, was the reason for all of this.

A massive object, roughly egg-shaped and maybe 50 meters tall, stood upright and perfectly still. Its surface was the purest, deepest black I had ever seen in my life, and it reflected no light at all. This created the uneasy effect of making the object seem two-dimensional when viewed from a still position, and it was only after observing it from another angle that you realized it was not.

The Egg (as it was quickly named), wasn't exactly shaped like an egg, per se. Its general shape was similar, yes, but the proportions were much different. This object was skinnier, more closely resembling a cross between a chicken's egg and a torpedo. The object stood upright on its own without the help of any sort of visible support, yet its bottom-most portion barely touched the ground, as if it was trying to be gentle with the earth below it.

I must have been standing there staring for a while, because I realized at some point that someone had been repeating my name with increasing impatience.

"Doctor Hart? My name is Colonel Betts, nice to meet you. I know this is a lot to take in, but please, this way," he said as he motioned quickly in his direction. He turned and began to walk briskly. "We need to get to work. Our time table's pretty strict here," and with that I was led into the hard-plastic habitat acting as the site's main science building.

We made our way down some short, narrow hallways past assorted armed guards and finally into what I could only presume was the operations center. A few dozen people moved around the room busily, while others sat typing away at computer stations. I was then hurried into our final destination: a cold, square room in the back of the hab that already contained a handful of others.

"Alright, folks, attention right here," the Colonel spoke with an authority clearly demonstrating his position as ranking officer. He then gestured towards me. "This is Doctor Samuel Hart, physicist. He'll be leading your team. You've got two goals here: What is it? Where'd it come from? And when I say the pressure is on your team, I mean it," he remarked with a tone that made some of the others in the room visibly nervous. "You don't just have the country watching...you have the entire world watching. Don't let them down. They are looking to you now for answers. But first, let's get you all up to speed."

III: What We Knew Then

"At roughly 1300 hours yesterday, Homeland received an unsubstantiated report of a mysterious object from local authorities. The object, which is now being referred to as the Egg, had appeared without notice or detection where you now see it. It was originally discovered by a group of mountaineers who reportedly frequent the area and had only just been up this pass and in this clearing 2 days prior." Colonel Betts paused briefly, letting the information sink in with the eight of us staring wide-eyed back at him. All of this had been on the morning news, though, and you'd have to have been quite literally living under a rock to have not heard about it, yet the sudden reality of it felt like a crushing weight. It was on every news station, outlet, and social media platform in the world, but being there, listening to him talk...it's hard to describe how truly lost we all felt. Nonetheless, we all nodded that we were following, and he continued.

"Reports like this, things like UFOs and unexplainable phenomena, come in all the time from around the world, but this one was unique; it was reported by almost a dozen independent sources over the course of the two hours following the initial sighting, with three of the sightings having been by low-flying plane. After being confirmed by local police and a government liaison, we were called in. As I'm sure each of you saw on your way up, the pass has been shut down in both directions, and an almost five-mile perimeter has been set up. No foot traffic, no vehicles, no flights overhead, unless authorized of course. Additionally, all reporting parties have been detained for questioning." More silent nods.

"Over the course of the last eight hours we've learned, well, very little about the object. As far as we can detect, it exudes no electromagnetic radiation, no sound, there's no heat transfer, and it causes no measurable effects to its surroundings. We do know that it absorbs approximately 99 percent of all incident light.

"As much as we can tell or was reported before our arrival, it has not moved or opened in any way, and simple attempts to interact with it have proven pointless. There are no doors, no windows, no seams— the surface of the object appears to be one unbroken object. Beyond this, we know very little, but as you can imagine, the pressure to ascertain both its origin and its purpose is high. It was found on American soil, but the war for rights to study has already begun—world leaders are meeting as we speak, and they'll want more than "I don't know." As you can understand, we'll be strictly limiting calls and communication to anyone outside this base unless otherwise permitted. For right now, any new information needs to stay in-house.

"I will be your direct contact for anything you find. Any questions?" He stopped and was clearly unsurprised by the deafening silence. In only a few minutes, he had described phenomena that broke more known universal and physical laws than there were fingers in the room, and he had likely disproved the careers of every scientist standing in front of him in one way or another. A spectacled man to my right spoke up first.

"Am I the only one who suddenly has to vomit?" The shades of green on the faces around the room confirmed he was not. With a nod and a "good luck" from the Colonel, I quickly put on my thick winter coat and made my way back through the tunnels the way I had come.

Despite my naturally calm composure, I was freaking out. My breathing was fast and I couldn't calm the thunder in my chest. I suppose walking back out the door into freezing cold mountain air and a military compound surrounding what I could only vaguely assume was some sort of extraterrestrial object didn't help. Some part of me had hoped that I would walk outside and it would simply be gone, but there it stood. Pitch black and monolithic. This sort of event was the dream of every *Star Wars*-loving, science-breathing nerd like myself, but here and now, I was just terrified. Not terrified that the Egg would open up and pour out some savage alien army or pose any real threat to Earth, but terrified that I wasn't ready. How could you be?

I'd spent my life studying physics and the universe. I'd published a ton of papers about what the

universe *was*. I'd spoken confidently in front of
symposiums of hundreds of people, telling them what
we *knew* about the laws that governed everything, but
this? I was unqualified for this. Deeply and utterly
unqualified. But, I would do what I always did when I
was stressed, when I didn't know the answer to
something. I would work, I would bury myself in the
research, and I'd keep asking questions, because
honestly, what else was there to do?

IV: What We Know Now

This is what we learned during our first three weeks studying the Egg. As the Colonel had informed us, the Egg did in fact absorb almost all light, 99.981176 percent to be exact. And it's not just visible light. The Egg absorbed all electromagnetic radiation. Ultraviolet, infrared, radio, you name it—we'd throw it at the Egg and we'd never see it again.

This wasn't a completely novel technology, though. Companies have created sprays and materials by vertically aligning carbon nanotubes to produce similarly deep-black colors and effects, although certainly not to the same level of efficiency. In those cases, when light strikes the material, instead of bouncing off, it becomes trapped and is continually deflected amongst the tubes. Eventually it's absorbed and dissipated as heat in the object. That's where the Egg was different and provided one of its bigger mysteries. When it absorbed the light, the Egg's temperature never increased like when you wear a black shirt on a hot summer day. Its surface always remained at the exact same temperature as the air, changing in-sync with atmospheric conditions and the day-night cycle, almost as if it could anticipate the changes before they happened. After hundreds of years of concrete, accepted theory, we watched the laws of thermodynamics and conservation of energy break down before our eyes.

Additionally, because it absorbed all electromagnetic radiation, it prevented us from scanning it in any way, which meant we had no way to tell what, if anything, was inside.

The material of the Egg itself was another mystery. It was seemingly invulnerable—at least against any attempts to take samples using any of our own tools —so testing the chemical composition of the object was impossible. That, in combination with its strange ability to regulate its temperature as efficiently as it did meant that the material was of no composition natural to Earth.

We also took a cue straight from what was, ironically, my favorite film, *Close Encounters of the Third Kind*, by attempting to rouse a response from the object using sound. Playing musical cues felt a little too on the nose for me, but we tried it, amongst other sounds across the spectrum. No response. No fun, climactic moment where it joined us in some musical duet, signaling peace and neighborly communication.

Amongst an assortment of other curiosities, there was one so obvious yet so confusing that no one seemed to want to approach it. How did it get here? Logistically speaking, assuming it had some form of propulsion and even "flew" in the typical sense of the word, there were no signs of a landing anywhere in the clearing. There was no scorching of the earth, no windblown vegetation, nothing. It's as if it had just appeared here in this spot, and it very well might have for all we knew. The Egg was not detected by a single ground or satellite-based radar, although this could have been due to its ability to absorb the radar signals, much like how stealth bombers can do the same and remain hidden from detection. Unfortunately, we just had no real way to determine how it showed up right here where it did. And that was just the beginning of it. We had no clue *why*, a question we were far more apprehensive to try to answer.

As far as why it chose *this* location, we were equally confused. The Egg decided on a fairly inhospitable place to land, at least by the standards of Earth-life, so there was no discernible merit from its choice. There wasn't much of anything besides rock, assorted yet common mineral types, and some dead weeds here and there.

The atmosphere was thin and cold at this elevation, so if they were looking for a rich supply of oxygen or nitrogen they chose a poor locale. There was an abundance of water, sure, in the form of ice and snow, but, on a planet that was seventy-one percent covered in water, having to do work to melt it down seemed inefficient. And that's under the conjecture that water was even what they wanted. A hostile alien force coming down and stealing the world's supply of water may have been the plot to far too many B-science fiction movies, but here and now, it seemed like as much a fiction as it was on the screen. And this was assuming they wanted anything from us at all.

By the end of the first few weeks, my team and I had found more that we simply couldn't explain or didn't understand than questions we had managed to answer. The more time that we spent working on the problems, the more that time itself didn't seem to exist in the same way. Days and nights flowed into each other and it seemed as though we were getting no closer to any real answers. It was clear that time could be acutely felt by others, though, as the milling of the bureaucrats became more anxious as the days passed.

Our access to news and knowledge of the outside world was limited to curated, pitifully-redacted briefings at the beginning and end of the days, but each one told much the same story. Turmoil was brewing quickly. The world was walking along a tightrope, barely balancing, teetering on the edge of conflict as governments squabbled over what to do about the Egg. The UN Security Council had met almost immediately after the object appeared. Countries began feuding over the "ownership rights" to the object just as quickly. Who could study it, why it wasn't being moved to some demilitarized zone, why other countries weren't being updated with new information. Understandable questions in a very inexplicable situation.

This was admittedly new territory for, well, everyone, so I suppose there wasn't a playbook on this sort of thing. Sure, it would have been nice to get some international help, even just on the research side, but I wasn't in charge. Every time I vocalized that thought to one authority or another, it was met with curt responses and excuses that "doing so could mean a breach of security and information." So, for the time being, we were alone, guarding and studying an object that was both a well-kept secret and the biggest news in the world. The feeling of the billions of eyes upon us as we conducted our fruitless studies, hoping we could bring some sort of salvation to the world's confusion, was perhaps more frightening than the Egg itself.

V: The Hum

The world shook me awake. The ground, my body, and the air itself seemed to vibrate. My head hurt from the pressure. Trying to follow the sound using the sound alone was impossible; it seemed to come from everywhere. Given that an object of presumably alien origin had recently appeared on Earth and was currently less than a hundred meters from where I lay, though, that was probably a good place to start. The compound's inhabitants seemed to have had the same idea, because, as I made my way through the hab and outside, it appeared as though the entire camp's population had emptied into the clearing and were now staring dumbfounded at the Egg.

The vibrations were being caused by a loud, albeit low pitched, sound emanating from the Egg. At least that was as much as anyone could assume. The hum was seemingly directionless, and it was also the least surprising of the two new changes to the Egg.

Instead of the pure black that we were thus far accustomed to seeing from the surface of the Egg, bright swirls of color were now present on its massive black exterior. They shifted, sparkled, and spiraled amongst the deep abyss, as if the Egg had become a giant, living marble. Because of the nature of the Egg's natural shade, it was impossible to tell whether we were seeing into it or if the colors were instead just moving along its surface. Regardless, the watching audience was enraptured. The many dozens standing around it, including myself, were utterly astounded. It was beautiful, unlike anything I had ever seen, like the Aurora Borealis multiplied tenfold shifting and undulating against a starless black sky.

The shocking change to what had thus far been a very static object had struck us all, but the sudden realization that this was the very first thing that had really happened since our arrival hit me like a truck.

"We're filming this right?" I shouted over the loud hum at the slack-jawed technician to my left.

"Never stopped!" he yelled back, pointing at a high bank of recently installed cameras while keeping his eyes on the Egg.

The colors, and their accompanying hum, persisted for what felt like an eternity. No one moved. No one did much of anything besides stare, motionless. The constant, droning sound seemed almost antithetical to the ever-changing, perceptibly random swirling of colors. Perhaps there was meaning in their duality, although it certainly wasn't apparent in that moment to all of us gawking at their existence.

And then, out of nowhere, after what may have been one minute or one-hundred, I was overcome by a sudden urge that to this day I cannot explain, and one that, in all honesty, seemed fairly opposite to the awe and confusion I felt in that moment. I *needed* to touch the Egg.

I slowly took one step, and then another, followed by more. Myself, and others, had touched the Egg many times before. It had been quickly determined to be safe and inconsequential, especially after most of the tourists and climbers who found it admitted they had touched it without any effect. However, right now, it seemed like an intrinsically terrifying thing to do. Yet, with assorted weaponry aimed at the object and some of the highest active military officials in the country staring at me with incredulity, I walked forward, right arm outstretched.

"Sir, the Doctor is moving towards the object! Orders? Do we restrain?" a soldier shouted towards the Colonel with his rifle barrel now aimed at me. The Colonel remained silent, or, if he had said anything in that moment, I didn't hear. If he had given a command, it must have been to stand down, because I reached out without being shot or tackled to the ground. Part of me hoped right then and there that the Egg would hatch its secrets for us all to know. Even an outpouring of little green men would have been a concrete answer to many of our questions. Nothing happened, however, and I placed my palm flat against the smooth surface, just as I had done many times before.

This time, something did happen. I felt an immense pressure explode throughout my body, and then the world went black.

VI: Aurora

The blue sky was filled with color as I stood in a large clearing, empty besides a thick layer of lush, bright green grass. Ribbons of blues and greens and reds and more billowed against the azure backdrop. The sun felt larger and brighter than I remembered, yet it was outshone by the aurora around it.

I couldn't help but feel awestruck, yet there was a nagging feeling, a sense that I didn't belong there. Something was trying to pull me away. I continued to stare up at the sky despite the pressure inside of me to move. It reminded me of a vast undulating ocean, one perpetually just out of reach.

The blue of the sky grew white, and it began to outshine the colors that swirled within it. An incredible hum erupted from all around me, loud in both my body and mind, and it too seemed to tug on me. It grew exponentially loud as the seconds passed, and then the world erupted into light.

I was startled awake. Someone's hand reached for me and helped me into a sitting position. I looked to my left into the eyes of Colonel Betts, who was sitting in a chair beside my cot. His face looked more tired than the stoic, hardened appearance I was more accustomed to. He had bags under his eyes and his face seemed to sag with worry.

"Are you alright, Doctor Hart? Doctor Hart?" I must have been staring.

"Yes, sorry, yes, I'm alright. Just a strange, vivid dream." I rubbed my eyes and straightened my back against the wall at the head of my cot. "What happened?"

"What do you remember, Doctor Hart?" It was then that I realized he was not the only one waiting for an answer. At the door of my small room stood the compound physician and psychologist, a few of my team members, and the peering eyes of perhaps a dozen others.

"Well, I remember walking up to the Egg, reaching out and touching it, and then I remember a surge of, I don't know, something."

"A surge of what? Electricity? Heat? Did it hurt? Can you explain it?" His eyes were desperately searching mine for an answer.

"No...no, or I don't know, maybe. I'm sorry; it's very difficult to explain. And everything went dark quickly. I passed out?"

"Yes," the Colonel said, "the moment you touched it you fell to the ground, unconscious." The viewing parties all seemed to stare at me in anticipation of an explanation I feared I didn't have. I sat for a moment to ponder the seemingly countless things that could have happened, and I suddenly realized that something seemed...missing. Something that had been there before.

"The hum is gone. Are the lights still there? Can I see?" I suddenly felt a great urgency. I placed my feet on the ground and started to stand, but the Colonel placed a firm hand on my shoulder and gently pushed me back down onto the bed.

"Doctor Hart," he hesitated, "the moment you touched the Egg, the moment you passed out...the hum, the lights...they both stopped. They haven't come back since." I looked back at him with obvious incredulity. Somehow, the act of me touching the Egg had turned off its light show. I felt both guilty and confused.

"Well I mean it's only been what, a few hours? There might be some sort of residual effects. I'd like to take a look," I said with more defiance than I intended.

"Sam," he said with soft pity, looking down. "It's been almost two days. You've been asleep for 40 hours."

"Two days! That thing knocked me out for two days?! Jesus Christ." I couldn't believe anything that was happening.

"That's not all the bad news!" said one of the peering eyes waiting at the door. I looked from them towards the Colonel expectantly, and he sighed, glancing frustrated in the direction of the comment.

"Yes, that's right," he said. "In the two days that you've been unconscious, quite a lot has changed. The world has gone, well, off its rocker. It's reached quite a tipping point. Many of the world's religions have responded to the Egg's existence. There have been countless reports of religious killings, mass suicides, and the like. Some believe that this is the second coming of Christ or the arrival of one God or another. Others think it's a sign of the rapture or the end of the world as we know it. Even the Vatican has released a statement saying that it's a sign that we must repent our sins before God hands down some sort of righteous justice." He rolled his eyes.

"Man...I mean we knew this might have happened at some point, right? Ultra-conservatives were responding right from the beginning," I said.

"But now the world's governments are noticing, and they are already tense enough. It's said that three quarters of the world's population believe in one faith or another. That's five or six billion people, and even if one half of a single percent of those people responded strongly, it would be noticed. It's causing a lot of tension around the world. Even more than there already was. Just in the last few days alone, there have been large-scale riots in New York, Paris, Moscow, Shanghai... everywhere. Our government just declared martial law in the capital. In goddamn D.C." *Martial law*? I knew I had only been out for two days, but it was hard to believe so much could happen in such a short amount of time.

"Jesus, that's pretty extreme. Why?" I asked.

"Between the riots and protests, the violence, and the bickering between our country and everyone else—and all those who are taking advantage of the disarray in one way or another—the government thought it best to start trying to impose some control before things get too out of hand—"

"Tell him about the Russians!" interrupted the same pair of eyes that had contributed a few moments ago.

"Alright, enough. Clear the room please. I'd like to speak to Doctor Hart in private." With that, one of the officers standing in the group at my door sighed and ushered everyone away. Colonel Betts and I were now alone.

"Doctor Hart...somehow, despite all of our precautions, video of you touching the Egg has leaked. It's everywhere, on every news station and website you can think of and on every one you cannot. We tried to contain the fire, to shut down every outlet's use of the video, but we just weren't fast enough." I looked at him flabbergasted and speechless. "We've detained the parties involved—a group of scared soldiers and a politician with his hands in too many people's pockets—but right now we're dealing with the fallout. You are now a household name, and you're also not very popular in the eyes of some very powerful people." He looked at me expectantly, hoping for some reaction that I simply couldn't give him. Unless he was looking for utter shock. I gave plenty of that.

"The Russians?" I finally muttered.

"They've released a statement criticizing our

supposed control of the object. They say it's not diplomatic or fair to the rest of the world to keep it to ourselves. They're using you as a prime example of that. 'American scientist first to interact with alien spaceship'. 'World left wondering what's going on.'" He paused for a few moments, clearly choosing his next words carefully. "At this point, I think they're probably right." I shrugged and nodded in agreement. "We never should have kept the Egg to ourselves. American machismo and selfishness at its finest, I suppose. Regardless, the race is on, Doctor. I'm not sure what the government really expects you to find, and honestly, I don't really care. Just find it. Before something more extreme happens." He stood and walked towards the door.

"Extreme? In what way?" I asked.

"Let's hope we never have to find out." He looked back at me steely-eyed, but with a worry that seemed far more commonplace around here by the day. He then turned and walked from the room.

VII: What's It All For?

The days began to move at a furiously increasing pace. The bustle of the camp grew, as did the nerves of its occupants. It had only been a month since the Egg had appeared, we were no closer to learning its purpose or origin, and yet the world around us seemed to be changing drastically in wait.

The pressure to learn something eye opening before the governments of the world started butting heads more *directly* was immense, but by the fourth or fifth week, we had almost entirely given up. The Egg had not come back to life since the day I had touched it, and we couldn't seem to explain why it had done it in the first place.

No significance was found in the hum, which resonated at a frequency of exactly 31 hertz. We correlated the frequency, timbre, decibel level, and just about everything else we could with every recorded or known source of sound that we could find, in hopes that maybe it was, if nothing else, trying to mimic something. It didn't seem to be communicating with us using sound, at least as far as we could tell.

The swirling colors were even more of a mystery. The pattern was completely random and never repeated exactly the same way. Although, we did discover one particular peculiarity. The colors moved through the entire spectrum of light visible to humans. The Egg had to have been conscious in that decision, to deliberately show us the entire range of colors that were specific to us as a species. Maybe it wanted to see how we would respond, or maybe it was some higher form of communication altogether. Maybe we were overthinking it all and it was simply saying *hi, we know who you are.*

At the end of another long day, I sat on the hard floor of the clearing, staring over the edge and down into the mountain valley below. I suppose I had spent so much time in my life looking up, so much time in the past few weeks looking up, that it had only just occurred to me that I hadn't taken much time to look down, to appreciate what was around me here on Earth. Perhaps that alone explained most of my past failed relationships, but I tried not to let my mind wonder too far in that direction.

After weeks of carrying an immense weight on my shoulders—the world watching, waiting, pressuring —sitting there in that moment felt quiet for some reason, perhaps the first quiet I'd ever truly experienced.

As I finished the horrible sandwich that had been rationed out to me for dinner, I began to feel a low rumble shake the ground beneath me, knocking loose snow into the dark valley beneath me.

I spun immediately, assuming the Egg had once again begun its colorful show, but it was still as black as night, and no one else seemed to notice the vibrations.

Just then, a large convoy of military vehicles crested the hill and rumbled into the clearing. This time, though, it wasn't just Humvees delivering or taking away VIPs. This time, the convoy also consisted of armored vehicles, anti-aircraft and heavy infantry weaponry, and personnel transports.

I stood and watched as the caravan filled much of the remaining space in the clearing. The transports were entirely empty aside from the drivers, which meant they weren't for transporting in. They were for transporting out.

As I considered the significance of the new arrivals, I made my way back into the science hab to ascertain if any of my team had made it any farther analyzing the video recordings. A sizable group of scientists, technicians, and soldiers were silently crowded around a large screen in the front of the room. I realized the cause of the huddle as I inched my way through the crowd. Either the information ban had been lifted or, more likely, one of the technicians had hacked their way around the protocols, because they had managed to bring up a news broadcast on the screen. It was the first true glimpse of the outside world that any of us had seen in weeks. The news anchor enunciated slowly and warily from her seat behind the desk.

"We have breaking news for you this morning. The Russian president has released another statement from the Kremlin in Moscow. The statement reads, and I quote, 'The Americans have harbored the alien object from the rest of the world's eyes, studying and evaluating it for more than a month now. They have hidden behind the false pretense that they are shielding the world from the dangers it may present, that they are only doing what is in their right and responsibility as one of the world's leading powers. Well today, we say 'no more!' We do not know what the object wants or what its purpose is on our planet. Yes, maybe it is an emissary for peace, but perhaps it brings with it nothing but destruction. Can we really be so arrogant to assume it has come all this way to befriend us? How can we truly learn how this affects the world if the world as a whole is not given the fair opportunity to study the object as one united people?

"'This is why today, a special council consisting of Russia, China, Brazil, Japan, France, the United Kingdom—as well as many other nations who have decided that enough is enough—have signed the AOR Accord. The Americans must give up access to the alien object in the next twelve hours, or we will have no choice but to remove it from them by force. It is our strong opinion that if the object cannot belong to the whole world, then it will belong to no one at all. Thank you, and may God be with us as we are all tested today."

The room was justifiably stunned. The anchor had said "this morning" which meant that what we saw wasn't live but was rather a recording that must have been stored in one government server or another. What was worse, was that we were now well into that twelve-hour window. Considering the massive, stockpiled convoy that had just arrived, I assumed the American president's answer had been a resoundingly clear *no*.

"Oh my god. What do we do now?" one of the scientists in the room asked, terrified. "We can't be safe here! Why haven't they evacuated us?"

"They must have been waiting for the President to make a decision before prematurely evacuating the camp," another answered.

As if perfectly timed, Colonel Betts pushed into the room hastily. "Grab your things, we're leaving, now!" he commanded.

"Sir, why've we waited this long to evacuate?" I asked.

"That's an excellent question, Doctor. It's one I'd like to know the answer to as well. Let's get off this rock first."

"How much time do we have?" I asked.

"Not enough," he said with an honesty that shook me. He waved me towards my room, signaling me to get my belongings, and made his way out the door as fast as he had come in.

VIII: Err on the Side of Selfish

With my backpack slung over my shoulder, I ran back through the now mostly vacant hab and out the front door. The compound was now a scene of what could only be described as structured chaos. Military personnel milled about quickly, shuffling scientists, bureaucrats, and others into the military transports. Equipment of all sorts was being abandoned and pushed aside as large weapons and armored vehicles were being moved into place, forming a sort of barricade around the Egg.

An officer who was near the door to the science hab directed me towards an idling transport near the exit to the clearing that had not yet been filled. I moved as fast as I could but was slowed by the crowds of shifting people. I pushed my way through the congestion and spotted the truck, which was now nearly full.

I climbed up the back and into one of the few remaining seats on the lengthwise benches that were attached to the transport's walls. Looking around at the people still moving around the camp, it was hard to believe they could possibly bring them all down in the remaining transports.

Some of the truck's passengers were talking amongst themselves, but some were deadly silent. I'm certain many of them simply wished they could somehow contact their loved ones.

I couldn't help but wonder what was going to happen as I sat there in wait. The sudden threat from the Accord members was, in reality, not that sudden. Tensions around the world had been high for weeks, and countries had been disagreeing the entire time about what should and needed to happen regarding the Egg. Sitting here now, though, being hastily removed from the mountain due to the threat of some sort of show of force just felt surreal. Would the Russians and their friends really come barging up the mountain with an army? This was all new to me, but I suppose it was new to everyone. Yet, here we were, and, for perhaps the first time since I'd gotten here, I really just wanted to go home. I didn't care about the Egg; I didn't care about the science. I just wanted to leave.

Colonel Betts climbed into the passenger seat of a Humvee across the clearing. I watched as his vehicle backed up, turned, and moved towards the top of the road exiting the clearing next to where our transport was idling.

That was when I heard it.

At first, I thought it was the sound of gases being released from an engine as a transport came to life and began its motion, but the sound continued longer than I would have expected. Its pitch started low, but it grew higher and louder, as if the source of the sound was growing closer. Louder and higher and then others began to notice and then I realized what it was, and before any of us could do anything there was a bright flash and then a massive pressure against the side of our truck, tipping it over and spilling its passengers.

The missile had struck only 10 or so meters to the right of our truck. The world seemed to reverberate around me as I hazily pulled myself off of an unconscious person and dragged myself slowly out of the flipped transport. Smoke filled the air to my left where the missile had struck a Humvee. What was left of Colonel Betts lay on the ground a short distance from the wreck.

I knew I had a concussion, but I pushed past it and tried to focus. I attempted to stand, faltered, then finally managed and moved in the direction of where the missile had hit. I could see survivors in various states of injury scattered about. I zeroed in on one close to me and ran towards them. A soldier lay crumpled and moaning, holding her hands on a wound in her leg.

"Keep the pressure on it!" I yelled as I grabbed her shoulders. I pulled her away from the fire and back in the direction I had come from. I could hear the turrets on one of the anti-aircraft weapons turn and then fire off a rocket from its chambers and into the air. Only moments later, the ground directly in front of us exploded in a mess of rock and debris. Both the soldier and I flew backwards from the explosion. I collided with the side of another of the transports, which now had people flooding out of it and running towards whatever cover they could find. The officer I had been pulling lay face down and unmoving a few feet away.

Despite the chaos, the screaming people, and the rocket fire, I realized in the break from explosions that I could hear the jet engines of fighters flying overhead. The anti-aircraft weapons fired off more rounds, and it was joined by more of the weaponry that had been brought up in the convoy. The mountain air roared with sound now and the ground shook with every shot fired off.

A third explosion ripped through the barracks hab at one end of the clearing. The barrack's storage was filled with an assortment of armaments, which added fuel to the proverbial and literal fire caused by the explosion. Secondary and tertiary explosions rang out from that area as ammunition and explosives were set off from the fire and heat. Not all of the ammunition stored in the barracks went off immediately, though. Some of it was thrown from the hab and acted like grenades as they hit things or flew through fire, creating additional havoc and destruction as they exploded across the clearing.

I dove out of the way and into cover behind a twisted chuck of metal as something red hot and fast flew by my head and lodged itself in a Humvee door a few dozen feet behind me. From over the barrier, I watched as a flaming case containing what I could only assume were grenade rounds or C4 flew in a high arc from the twisted barracks directly towards the group of vehicles and weapons firing upon the aircraft flying overhead.

"Hey! Watch out!" I shouted towards them. "It's going to explode! Move—" The crate erupted as it smashed against the side of one of the armored vehicles, instantly tearing holes in it and decimating the area around it. Even from many feet away and behind my small metal shelter, the heat from the blast seared my exposed skin. I could hear sharp thuds as shrapnel flew around the camp. One such sound was incredibly close.

I looked down at the metal barrier and saw a hole about waist high that wasn't there before. Then came the pain in my arm. I looked down and saw a three-inch piece of shredded metal sticking out of my right arm, just above my elbow. The pain was intense, but the heat of the object seemed to have cauterized the wound as soon as it entered, which, for the time being, would mean that I at least wouldn't bleed out.

I crouched as low as I could with my back against the barrier, holding my arm against my chest. The habs were mostly destroyed, the remaining few transports were covered in a soft canopy that would provide no protection, and most of the remaining vehicles, as far as I could see through the thick black smoke, were destroyed. My small metal barrier only really protected my back and part of my sides and my luck would soon run out. The missiles kept falling all around and there was no end in sight. I closed my eyes and waited for the end. Except, before the end ever came, something else did.

A low sound, existing and originating from

everywhere, could be heard and felt above the bangs and reverberations of the explosions around me. The Egg, which had previously been difficult to see through the dark smoke, was no longer hidden. It shone bright with swirling colors, undulating in the blackness, acting like a beacon in a dark, terrifying storm.

What were my options? Sit here and die? Or touch a giant glowing alien object and probably pass out and then die? Given the circumstance, I decided I'd take my chances with the alien object.

I wrenched myself upwards, fighting through the pain in my arm. The Egg was now far brighter than anything else was in the area, and I spun myself towards it, ready to move with everything I had. Flaming objects and debris littered my path but with one hand over my nose and mouth to block the smoke and the other held to my chest, I pushed forward. Explosions went off to my left and right, pushing my body here and there with each wave of pressure. With a final exertion, I lunged over a pile of rubble and what looked like a half-buried body in a military uniform and landed hard on the other side, just underneath the lower curve of the Egg. There didn't seem to be any damage at all to the Egg, which wasn't particularly surprising given our tests of its structural integrity.

The colors seemed to slowly amass on the Egg in the area closest to me. I stared at them for a moment, caught up in innate curiosity and fascination, but I could hear one of the jets approaching for another pass in the distance. With no other viable options, I looked up at the Egg, let out a brief sigh of resignation, and reached up and touched it.

IX: Humanity

What happened next is hard to describe, so I'll do my best. I was still outside among the destruction and fire, but I wasn't. I was standing in the location that the Egg had been, but the Egg was gone. I was elevated on some sort of smooth platform that seemed to be levitating quite a few feet in the air above the stone floor of the clearing. The platform was circular and approximately 30 feet in diameter, and I noticed something strange as I walked around it. The space seemed to be shielded from the outside. Explosions, fire, debris, and smoke were all blocked from entering and could be seen hitting an invisible barrier that surrounded me. The space seemed roughly cylindrical in shape and incredibly tall. I walked to the edge of the perimeter and touched the surface, which was perfectly smooth and entirely invisible.

All the signs were there, and it was obvious given the empirical evidence, but it still took me a few moments to realize that I was in fact standing inside of the Egg. Somehow, I was now inside of it and looking out.

The Egg's utter blackness suddenly made a lot of sense.

By absorbing all of the incident light, radiation, and energy from the outside, it could be perfectly transmitted and viewed from the inside. And by redistributing the energy on this side of the wall, they could mitigate the heat that came with energy absorption.

I couldn't help but be reminded of those one-way mirrors you'd see in interrogation rooms in cop dramas—the ones where the suspects in the room would just see themselves in a mirror, but police on the other side of the wall could stare through it like a window, watching the suspect. Except, in this case, we didn't see ourselves in a mirror on the outside but rather perfect blackness. The implications of the metaphor then dawned on me. *They were observing us.*

Were we the criminals and them the police? What reason would they have to come and watch us, to sit and to do nothing but watch? The thought made me queasy and uncomfortable, that they had been in this room, right where I was standing, observing us through their window. They watched us struggle to learn what we could about them, keeping the rest of the world at bay, only to descend into turmoil and violence. They watched humans bomb their own species indiscriminately, and they sat here as we bombed them as well. And where were they now?

I sat on the smooth floor and just watched as the flames of the outside continued to lick at the invisible walls and as the jets decided that the deed had been done and flew away, no longer needed. I watched as a platoon of soldiers appeared at the top of the hill in jeeps and armored vehicles. I watched them exit their vehicles, watched them stare in awe at the Egg, looking at me but not truly looking at me. I watched as they methodically moved through what remained of the compound, detaining those few who still survived. I sat, and I observed. Just as *they* had.

I couldn't help but cry. The tears came, and I let them. They received no fight from me as I sat broken, tired, confused, and angry. The tears must have come hard, because my view of the outside began to blur, to fade, and then it began to disappear altogether. The room grew dark and faded and I assumed I was blacking out for some reason, but I wasn't. The window was becoming opaque and my view of the outside world was being replaced by a wall.

It was smooth and of a similar material as the outside of the Egg, but, unlike the blackness of the outside, this wall was grey, and it had odd line-like markings running vertically the entire height of the Egg. Despite the dark colors of the wall, the massive inner portion of the Egg, which was a single cavernous room, was fairly well illuminated. That being said, I couldn't see anywhere that the light could be coming from. Perhaps it emanated from the walls themselves, as the thin veins running up them seemed to pulsate with a dull white light.

The room was empty with the exception of two large, cylindrical objects on opposite sides of the room from each other. Their backs seemed molded to the

Egg's walls. They were completely opaque and had the same veins on their surface, but, as I walked closer to one of them, its lights seemed to pulsate more slowly. I stopped in front of it and ran my hand along one of the veins. The surface material seemed to change, slowly growing brighter and then becoming transparent altogether. The cylinder seemed to be a container of sorts, but the object that it contained horrified and confused me. I couldn't help but stumble backwards in shock when it came entirely into view.

Inside the container, floating naked in a stagnant fog, was a human woman. Her eyes were closed, and she didn't seem to respond at all to my presence, but she was breathing, albeit slowly. Her arms and legs were slightly pulled up and close to her body in a half-fetal position, and in that moment, she reminded me of a baby, suspended in its mother's womb, waiting to be birthed into the world.

I turned towards the other cylinder and touched it, waiting for the surface to become transparent so I could confirm my suspicion. As expected, a human man floated inside, peacefully unaware of the catastrophe and violence and strife of the world outside his existence.

Where had they come from? Were they taken? Abducted? They seemed so perfect and pure, unblemished and unburdened by existence in the outside world. If they had been taken, it was from a life of solitude and safety not easily found on Earth.

So that would mean what? That they originated

with the Egg? They came to Earth? By all theories of evolution of life as we knew it, that was entirely impossible. Yet here they were, breaking so many of those rules just as the Egg had already done to so many others.

The surfaces of both cylinders darkened, and after a short time they were once again opaque, and I was once again alone. The Egg was silent. No explanation, no hum, no nothing.

"What do you want?!" I yelled upwards at nothing. "Why am I here? Why are you showing me any of this?" I realized I was screaming. "I didn't ask for this! I don't want it!" My voice echoed throughout the chamber but received no response. Then the world started going dark, and, this time, I knew I was blacking out for real.

X: Where We Came From and Where We're Going

Our military Humvee moved quickly along the thin mountain pass. Snowdrifts on both sides narrowed the road down to a single lane, assuming it was anything more than that to start. The mountain face rose dozens of meters on our right and disappeared into the clouds above. On the left, there was nothing but a sheer drop into the foggy nothingness of the mountain valley below.

I was sitting in my office less than eight hours before. Now I was being rushed up a mountain thousands of miles away with a knot in my stomach and a deep uncertainty for what would come next. I was moving away from the comfort of my life, the comfort in the fact that I understood everything about it. I was leaving that solace and moving towards all that came next. My confidence in the world told me I would be fine, but some part of me fought against that with an anxiety that I couldn't help but allow permeate through me as we made our way up the mountain. Maybe it was nervousness for the future, or maybe it was the ease of what came before that I was really so unsure of.

"Doctor Hart. Doctor Hart, sir...we are almost at the site," said the uniformed officer in th ,e, humor me. Where are we going right now?" I asked.

"Yes sir. We are on our way to the staging site. You have been requested as a consultant at the site, to study the object," he responded. A voice came quietly over his radio as he was addressing me. He reached down to check it but was interrupted by another of my questions.

"The object?" I asked. *Sergeant Johnson, we have a situation here! Johnson, come in*, his radio crackled loudly.

"Yes sir, they think it may not be from this world," he said, ignoring his radio but clearly answering me with the curt politeness of someone whose focus was truly needed elsewhere.

Then, like a tidal wave, it all hit me at once. The Egg. The weeks studying it, researching. Colonel Betts. Passing out. The Russians. The Attack. And then a lot that I couldn't quite explain. Here I was, again, driving up the mountain to do it all over. We were heading up to our doom. Before I could stop myself, I was shouting.

"We have to stop! We can't go up there!" I yelled towards the front seat. The voice came over the radio again and this time its tone was far more urgent.

"I'm sorry, why is that, sir? Please, Colonel Betts is expecting us," the officer said with an ever-growing irritation in his voice.

"If we go up there you will all die! Every one of you! The Russians will attack, they will kill you all, and they will try to destroy the Egg! This is all wrong!" I was grabbing the man's lapel now, and he grabbed my wrist hard, pulling it off him with a force justified by my outburst.

"Doctor, if you do not calm down I will have no choice but to restrain you—" He was interrupted by the soldier in the driver seat.

"We're pulling up to the site now, sir." We made our way over the hill at the top and entered the clearing. The camp was situated just as I had remembered it. The habs were all in their rightful places and the military vehicles sat along the circumference of the large clearing. Except, unlike the last time, the camp's staff didn't seem to be busy milling about. They were not working; they were not talking. They were all just standing, mouths agape, and staring. Staring straight up, straight up to where the Egg used to be.

Now, there was nothing.

The center of the clearing was empty.

And, at that moment, I couldn't help but feel nervous. Nervous for what was to come, and nervous for what had come before.

Acknowledgements

If anyone ever tells you writing is easy, they're lying. I came into this project with a head full of ideas and absolutely no clue how to do any of it. Turning those ideas into something coherent and enjoyable was infinitely more difficult than I could have imagined, and I suppose I still don't really know if I succeeded in that. What I do know is that I would have undoubtedly failed if it wasn't for the help and support of a few people.

Most significantly, I want to thank my partner, Melanie. She never complained about how much this claimed my time, she always listened to my ramblings and silly ideas, and she tolerated the whole process with a patience and grace that was both endearing and deeply generous. She always reminded me that no matter how the book came out, I'd always have at least one fan. She was, is, and always will be a source of laughter and unabashed joy in my life, and for that I will be eternally grateful. Thank you, Mels.

I'd also like to thank Andy, one of my closest long-time friends. He was kind enough to provide this book with its incredible artwork and cover. I'm also indebted to him for simply letting me talk to him about the book itself. Our conversations were immensely valuable in helping me fine-tune ideas and further refine the book's tone as a whole. Thanks for being such a reliable and incredible friend, even from across the planet or a country.

Thank you to the rest of my close friends and family, for always supporting these silly creative pursuits and for not telling me that they are as much a waste of time as they sometimes feel. I appreciate it all. Without these people, none of this would exist, so it is as much their book as it is mine.

Lastly, even though they will likely never see this, I want to thank the filmmakers, authors, musicians, and artists that I've so thoroughly enjoyed in my life. The crazy, bold, interesting, scary, and wonderful stories that they told and continue to tell in their mediums have influenced every aspect of this book, in ways both big and small, and it is because of them that I do this at all. This book is my attempt at contributing to a community of storytelling that these people altogether revolutionized for the better.

Oh, and I'd like to thank our dogs, Luna and Vega. I'd like to thank them just for existing.

About the Author

Dillon Sienko is a software engineer, musician, and self-published author with degrees in astronomy and computer science. He also has a long-time love of film and literature. Dillon is devoted to giving his readers thrilling and cinematic stories motivated by science, technology, and the real world, but also stories heavily influenced by the countless science fiction movies he watched growing up in western Massachusetts. He now lives outside of Sacramento, where he's still watching movies. For more information on Dillon and his work, visit www.dillonsienko.com.

If you liked what you read (or even if you didn't), consider leaving a review at your preferred retailer (or anywhere you hang out online). Your feedback is immensely important to me, and it helps other readers decide if this book is right for them.